GREAT LIVERMERE
NORTON
BURY
ST EDMUNDS
WOOLPIT
STOWMARKET
LAVENHAM
MARY
March 4th
1979
BENTLEY
N
W
E
S

AN

ANTHOLOGY

Suffolk Haunts

Original Stories Inspired by the Legends and Landscapes of East Anglia

Foreword by award winning novelist Polly Crosby

First edition 2024

ISBN: 978-1-9989996-5-1

Published by the University of Suffolk Talking Shop Press,

Waterfront Building, 19 Neptune Quay, Ipswich IP4 1QJ

https://www.uos.ac.uk/courses/pg/ma-creative-and-critical-writing

Welcome to our 2024 anthology *Suffolk Haunts: Original Stories Inspired by the Legends and Landscapes of East Anglia.* This is the fourth in our highly successful series of anthologies of original stories from the Creative and Critical Writing postgraduate students at the University of Suffolk. These anthologies of new writing all focus on the importance of place in storytelling. Each short story is set in and inspired by a specific location and aims to bring to life the complex and layered traces and connections we have with each other and with our landscapes. In doing this, our writers also illustrate the ways literature has such a vital role in our county's cultural traditions: past, present, and future.

Our first and much-loved anthology *Suffolk Folk* took local myth and folktales as inspiration, while the second anthology *Suffolk Arboretum* looked at the ancient trees and woodlands of the county. *Suffolk Reflections* brought an imaginative focus to the inland and coastal waters of the region.

This new anthology *Suffolk Haunts* connects us to the stories that come to us long after the sun has set – stories that speak softly from the shadows of forgotten memories and dreams. In this collection, you will find ghost stories to make you smile and laugh, alongside stories of superstition, human fears and desires. Stories that speak of those who long to forget and those who long to remember; stories that speak of things done and things that have come undone. From friendly ghosts in thriving public houses to forgotten letters and mysteries in museums, from a chilling account of ghost story writer M.R. James as a boy to a glamorous movie star that haunts an old cinema, here are the stories that blow the winds of winter and the heat of summer nights right through us. These original tales show us what it is to be haunted by the ghosts of what has been, what might have been, and what might never be.

Suffolk Haunts includes an introduction to each story along with directions, so that it is possible to visit every location in the anthology. In fact, we recommend you enjoy a tour of our beautiful county of Suffolk with the anthology in hand!

As an addition to the anthology, we have also included the winning and shortlisted entries from the Student New Angle Prize 2024. This award, now in its tenth year, is offered by the Ipswich Institute which runs the national *New Angle Prize*, and the *Creative Suffolk Author Award* sponsored by the University of Suffolk. These competitions celebrate writing that evokes the rich and varied cultural landscapes of Suffolk and the talented writers who live and work here.

We would like to thank Jane Dixon Smith for her help with book design and formatting, Chrissie Nicholls of Inkpot & Pen for the beautiful end-paper maps, and everybody who worked on this book. Thank you to Dr Lindsey Scott, Course Leader for the MA Creative and Critical Writing, for the focus of this anthology, and MA student Sarah Waterson, for all her work in helping to edit and collate the collection. A big thank you also goes to East Anglian novelist Polly Crosby for the foreword to the collection. Finally, a huge congratulations to all our writers for their wonderful and haunting stories.

Dr Amanda Hodgkinson
Associate Professor English and Creative Writing
University of Suffolk

Introduction by Polly Crosby

Suffolk is a landscape saturated with myth and folklore, a place touched by creeping, melancholic beauty. It is a county of haunting tales and ethereal stories, which, once heard, stay with you forever.

As a Suffolk-born girl, brought up on the coast at Walberswick, my blood runs with the salt from the sea and the mud from the marshes. As a child, I spent so much time outside that sometimes I felt like part of the landscape, my hair braided with reed feathers, a necklace of oyster shells and Sanderling feathers at my neck. Ever since, wherever I have lived in the world, I can still taste the salt smack of samphire on my tongue, still feel the wet sting of sea breeze on my cheeks.

A place you love never leaves you, and the same can be said for a story that you love: you carry both with you all of your life. It is impossible not to take inspiration from such a place as Suffolk. For me, it is embroidered into my heart. We writers are magpies, stealing names, places and people and stitching them together in an intricate, living, breathing patchwork. My love affair with Suffolk began when I was a child, and it has only grown, surging like a spring tide, spreading like cuckooflower on a water meadow.

When I first began trying to write a novel at the tender age of nineteen, I looked to the countryside around me for inspiration. Many of my novels are set in a fictionalised version of Suffolk: a ghostly, ethereal landscape filled with echoes of the past. Of course, *all* writing is fictionalised, just as all paintings are an artist's impression. I rarely name the place I'm writing about, but with every word I write, the county's essence is imprinted in the story, just as an echo of my fingerprints strokes each key of the laptop. I can smell Suffolk and taste it in the air as I work, catching fistfuls of it and bringing it to my nose to inhale. When I write, I gorge on the world around me, the vast skies and the endless rivers and streams. My writing borrows from my childhood, from stories whispered over campfires on the beach: the crumbling cliffs at Dunwich, with bleached white skulls tumbling from old graves; the Cathedral of the Marshes at Blythburgh, its faded grandeur holding so much wealth and poverty and violence. And Walberswick, always Walberswick, beloved of artists and writers, of film stars and musicians. A muse for so many.

For what is the setting of a story, if not a muse? It is a character in itself. Gothic tales are nothing without the world they inhabit. The most chilling of ghosts, the most unnerving of monsters will not be convincing if you do not tether them to a believable world. Without a place to haunt, they are simply wisps of the writer's imagination.

In this wonderful anthology, we are introduced to so many Suffolk locations. Abbeys and priories vie with reservoirs and rivers, villages and towns abut wild gardens and ancient lanes. So many different places, so many different layers. So many different stories. Yet there is one link that unites them all: the dark and delicious seam that runs hauntingly through each and every story's heart.

Contents

The Angel Hotel, Lavenham by Gabrielle Stones 1
The Landladies of Lavenham 2

Moyse's Hall Museum by Ellen Freeman 6
Miss Mary 7

The Abbey Gardens, Bury St Edmunds by Joel Pank 12
The Abbey Watcher 13

Great Livermere by Muriel Moore-Smith 18
In Heaven and Earth 19

St Andrew's Church, Norton by Heather Rugg 24
The Graveyard, the Girl, and the Gift 25

Woolpit by Jayd Green 31
Agnes Barre of St Martin's Land 32

Stowmarket by Molly Britton 36
Miss Morton, You're Needed on Set 37

Bentley Village by Jessica Spence 44
The Monk of Dodnash Priory 45

Alton Reservoir at Tattingstone by Sarah Waterson 50
Going Home 52

Christchurch Mansion, Ipswich by Rose Dawn 58
The Library 60

The Woolpack, Ipswich by Alec Taylor 65
Admiral Grog 66

Ipswich Waterfront by Chris Odogwu 71
Withered Roses 72

St Mary-le-Tower Church, Ipswich
by Daniel Snowling 76
When the Music Stops 77

The River Orwell by Roy Haddock 82
Nightmare on the Orwell 83

Felixstowe Landguard Fort by Elise McManus 88
The Ghost Tour 89

Butley Priory by Amber Atkinson 94
The Ghost Room 95

Orford Ness by Caroline Roberts 103
Taken by the Sea 104

Rendlesham Forest by Mike Laurence 108
Rendlesham Forest, 1993 110

Framlingham Castle by Milena Ristic 115
Come Closer 116

Blythburgh by Jeni Neill 121
The Yellow Ribbon 123

Blythburgh by Lou Mary Carr 128
The Wonder 130

Dunwich by Matthew Wiles 135
The Vanishing 136

Covehithe by Rob Sadler 141
Tides of Covehithe 142

Lowestoft by Sheena McCallum 146
First Light 148

Student New Angle Prize 2024 **152**

Colours of Our Days by Jeni Neill
(Winner of the SNAP Prize 2024) 153
Colour of Our Days 155

Wenhaston's Doom by Lou Mary Carr
(Runner-up of SNAP 2024) 158
Wenhaston's Doom 160

Rooted by Sheena McCallum 163
Rooted 164

The Habitat by EJ Daniels 167
The Habitat 168

Shingle Street by Harriet Sellers 171
Shingle Street 172

You Can't Hold Back the Sea by Tracy Davies 175
You Can't Hold Back the Sea 176

Writer Biographies 179
Creative Writing at the University of Suffolk 189
Other MA Creative and Critical Writing student
anthologies available from The Talking Shop Press 190

The Angel Hotel, Lavenham by Gabrielle Stones

In the heart of Lavenham sits the Angel Hotel. The first time I visited, I just knew there were stories to tell. Surrounded by independent businesses and small shops, the Angel Hotel adopts the same welcoming nature, inviting you in with its warm atmosphere and captivating architecture. I could visualise my story as soon as I stepped inside.

Follow the A1071, until you reach Lavenham. Go past Market Lane, and make sure to take in all of the surroundings. Located behind the Market Cross proudly stands the Angel Hotel. Make your way inside and be welcomed by the staff, enjoy a drink, and soak up the atmosphere.

The Landladies of Lavenham

The pub bell chimes through the square, roars of cheering follow. Bar staff are pulling pints with grins painted on their faces, tinsel wrapped around their jumpers. The Christmas tree in the corner of the pub is illuminating the room, shining through the empty glasses that are building up on the various surfaces. Used Christmas crackers are scattered over tables and under chair legs, accompanied by repeats of crumpled up jokes and a multitude of plastic games. People are endlessly ordering drinks.

'I'll have another glass of your house wine.'

'Top up, please!'

'Go on then, another won't hurt.'

There are stained circles on the bar from the conveyor-belt of glasses making their way around. Behind the bar is a door, and beyond it are drinks crates and barrels. There is a woman in the doorway, smiling back at the crowded bar. She is petite, her light orange hair in ringlets. She wears thick makeup; a sturdy eyeliner and a red lipstick smeared across her mouth. She has a twinkle in her eye, soaking up the festive atmosphere that is embracing the pub. She steps out, avoiding the chaos of the bar staff. Families are gathered, party hats tilted, their drinks swaying in their hands whilst they talk.

'Don't be shy, drink! It's Christmas,' the landlady chimes, waving her arms in the air. She leans towards a man with wisps of grey through his beard. He is wearing a garish yellow Christmas jumper and is talking to a young girl who is sitting opposite him, slurping on an apple juice.

'Well, you always picked the most hideous jumpers, Graham!' she chuckles, focusing her attention on the young girl.

'This is never your Harriet? Oh, my word,' she gasps, admiring the young girl's brunette bob and dazzling brown eyes. 'She's the spit of your Polly.' The landlady shakes her head in disbelief before making her way up the bar, smiling at the crowds of people all around.

'Don't sit with an empty glass. There should be no empty glasses in the room!' she yells, grinning at more people coming through the door, leaving their frosted coats on the nearby pegs.

The roar in the room suddenly gets louder as a young lady walks through from behind the bar with a similar shade of orange hair. She rings the large brass bell to the right of her, swinging its rope to make it chime loudly all around the pub.

'Drink up, as the next ones are free!' She beams as the customers cheer, racing to the bar to give their orders. The older lady watches, observing the people all around her. She grunts and makes her way to the bar taps.

The younger lady is pouring drinks.

'Nothing like a bit of festive cheer, 'ay Graham?' she beams, placing his full pint of Guinness on the bar.

'Ah yes, your Gran was full of that!' He chuckles, wearing a thick cream moustache after his first gulp.

'I still am, Graham!' the older lady responds, leaning for the pump. Her hand floats through it as she tries to grasp it with her hand. 'I can still pour drinks and bring a festive cheer to everyone!'

She sighs, tirelessly trying to grasp the beer pump.

The younger woman is still full of laughter and pulling the pumps effortlessly.

'Oh, what use is it?' The older lady scowls, disappearing out the back, the sound of the festivities blending in the distance. She shuffles around, looking at all the pictures hung on the walls. She hears the bar bell ring again and looking through the crack of the door to the bar, she sees a wine glass raised in the air.

'Now, Christmas is celebrated largely around here,' the younger landlady says loudly, and her words are followed by a huge roar.

'Yes, yes, we all agree,' she continues. 'And no Christmas is complete without family and friends. We want to thank all of you for continuously being here over the festive period, but I also want to thank someone very special. I want to thank my dear Granny Rae.'

The older lady beams and heads closer to the door.

'Without her, this pub would not be half of what it is today, and a lot of you probably wouldn't be standing here now. She was the definition of a landlady, and she is everything I aspire to be. So, if we could all raise a glass to Granny Rae.'

As one voice, the pub-goers cheer and everyone clinks their glasses.

'We also wouldn't be walking home sober!' somebody roars from the back.

The crowd in the pub laugh loudly, and the older lady watches. She feels a great sense of pride wash over her.

It would always be her pub; living or not.

Moyse's Hall Museum by Ellen Freeman

'Miss Mary' was inspired by the witch trials which took place in Bury St Edmunds in 1645. While my story is fictional, the real Mary Everard was one of sixteen women and two men who were executed by the Witchfinder General, Matthew Hopkins.

In 2023, I visited Moyse's Hall Museum in Bury St Edmunds for the first time and was instantly inspired to write about this event in local history. The witch trials are still misunderstood in many ways, making the work that museums such as Moyse's Hall do to inform people of these histories, all the more important.

If you're interested in local history and you'd like to know more about the witch trials in East Anglia, particularly in Bury St Edmunds, I would highly recommend you visit.

And if you do, make sure to keep an eye on the time!

Miss Mary

Mary Everard had never felt quite so desperate for her lunchtime walk. The rain pounding against the shop window only made it worse. The very second that twelve o'clock arrived, Mary rushed down the stairs, weaved between the bookshelves and dashed out of the front door. Her umbrella had turned inside out the last time she had tried to use it, so she tugged her hood up and headed towards the bakery.

She had been working part-time at her uncle's bookshop for just over a month, and she found herself looking forward to her lunchtime trips to her favourite bakery. This time of year, she found that the streets were particularly quiet. Nobody seemed to want to brave the rain, but stormy weather had always been one of Mary's favourite things. As a child, she would stay up watching lightning crack across the sky, her heart thumping, and her eyes wide as her sister hid beneath her bed.

Today was no different. The streets were silent, the only sounds were Mary's heels clicking against the wet cobblestones and the pouring rain. She wrapped her coat a little tighter around her as rainwater dripped from her hood, landing with a splash on the tip of her nose. Mary loved the rain but as she reached the bakery, she couldn't help but look up at the sky as she tried to remember the last time she had seen the sun shining.

'Your usual?'

A bright voice brought her back to the present. The bakery's manager stood behind the till, covered in flour, sugar and icing.

Mary nodded, pushing back her hood, and smiled.

Hot chocolate and freshly made pizza in hand, Mary found herself wandering through the streets towards the old abbey. She knew she should head back to the shop where it would be warm and dry, but she had missed her mid-morning break, and now she had a whole hour-and-a-half to avoid customers and her uncle's terrible jokes. As she admired the remains of the abbey – it had always fascinated her – she spotted a bench protected from the rain by the biggest tree she had ever seen. She couldn't believe she had never noticed it before.

Mary settled onto the bench, unwrapping her pizza, and sipping her hot chocolate. She watched a squirrel chase another squirrel around the ruins. Something rustled beside her and as she turned, expecting another squirrel to have appeared, she saw an envelope caught under a stone, half tucked under the bench. As Mary bent to retrieve it, her hand stopped. The writing on the envelope was faded, the ink smeared and running from the rain, but the name was unmistakable. She couldn't have missed it. She had seen it almost every day.

Miss Mary Everard

Mary shivered, her hand still frozen mid-reach. A part of her didn't want to touch the envelope. But the same part of her that loved thunderstorms and lived for that prickly feeling on the back of her neck snatched the envelope up before she could change her mind.

Tearing it open, she frowned. A ticket to Moyse's Hall

Museum had been tucked inside. There was no note, nothing to indicate who had left it there.

Biting her lip, she debated whether this had been an entirely innocent, if slightly spooky, coincidence. Perhaps there was another Mary Everard living in Bury St Edmunds who had just happened to sit here earlier in the day? And who had, for some unknown reason, kept a ticket to a local museum in an envelope with her name on it. Mary shivered again. No, someone had left this here for her to find. She didn't know who or why, or even how they had known she would come to the abbey, but if there was one thing Mary did know, it was that she could never say no to a spooky coincidence.

Moyse's Hall Museum was as quiet as the rest of the town. Mary handed the ticket over at the entrance before slipping the now empty envelope into her coat pocket. She loved souvenirs.

Mary had lived in Bury St Edmunds for almost ten years but had never been to this particular local attraction before. In all honesty, she hadn't really known it existed. She had walked past it countless times but had never noticed it before. As she entered the second floor of the museum, Mary realised that if she had known about this place, she would have spent much more time here. The room was filled with memorabilia relating to historic local criminals, as well as the local witch trials.

The rain had intensified, and Mary could hear it slamming against the roof of the building. The wind howled outside. Rainwater dripped from her coat onto the floor.

Checking her watch, she froze. Quarter past twelve. She shook her head, pulling her phone from her coat pocket: 12:15pm. But she had left the shop at least forty-five minutes ago. It could have been closer to an hour. The prickly feeling on the back of her neck was back.

Desperate to distract herself, Mary turned to the witchcraft exhibition. She scanned the story of the trials, her eyes lingering on the assortment of related artefacts kept safely behind the display glass. She tried *not* to look too closely at the book to her right, which looked as if it were made of skin. Instead, she focused on the story of the trials. She was familiar with them, of course, having grown up fascinated by all the country's witch trials. A clock struck the hour somewhere in the distance, just as her eyes caught on a name at the bottom of the list of local witch trial victims.

Miss Mary Everard.
Sentenced to death for the crime of witchcraft.
Mary Everard died at 12pm, alongside many others.

There was a buzzing in Mary's head. Her vision blurred as she pulled her phone from her pocket with shaking hands: 12:00pm. The same time her namesake, so many years before, had died. Before Mary could turn for the door, the room fell into darkness, and she slumped to the floor.

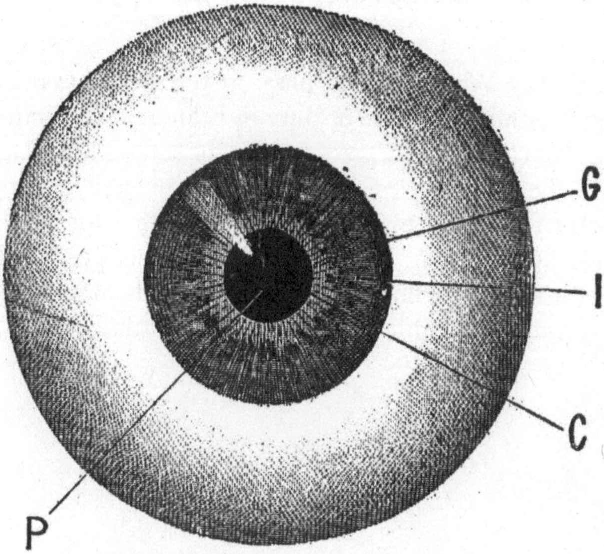
G
I
C
P

The Abbey Gardens, Bury St Edmunds by Joel Pank

'The Abbey Watcher' takes place in the Abbey Gardens located within the centre of Bury St Edmunds. Inspiration came from a visit to the gardens after the sun went down, in which the otherwise tranquil space became eerily gloomy, which I felt would make for a perfect setting for a short horror piece. The story takes place from the perspective of a narrator who has a horrifying encounter with an unknown entity after finding himself in the park after dark.

The Abbey Watcher

The week had been long. My head was throbbing, and I could feel another migraine coming on. I just needed to get out for a while. Pry my eyes away from the screens, the meetings, the petty dramas, and the family feuds. I just wanted to be somewhere else for a while.

I found myself going to the Abbey Gardens almost a dozen times a month, so I headed there again that day. My routine mostly consisted of walking laps around ruins and flower beds, seeing how much the roses and buttercups had grown, then getting myself a chocolate ice-cream and unwinding on a bench somewhere for the next hour.

This time, it was a bench just across the maze of ruined walls by the play area, overlooking the river. I remember the cold air being bitter, but the sun shining against a clear sky made the gardens busier than usual. Despite being in the presence of so many people, I couldn't shake a strange feeling that had been welling up inside me since I had entered the park. Like a fifth sense going haywire within me, though for what reason at the time, I couldn't tell. Somehow, it just felt like I had drawn the attention of something ethereal. What happened, between the me pondering the thought and the rapid setting of the sun is lost on me. Had I fallen asleep? No, surely someone would have woken me. There was a gap in my memory, as if someone had spliced a small period of time out of a film reel. I was surrounded by the chatter of people walking by and the playful laughter of children across from me.

Then I blinked, and suddenly the sun vanished, and all sound was snuffed out, leaving nothing but a damning silence. Nightfall hadn't completely rolled in yet, meaning my surroundings were dimly lit by a dark blue light.

I rubbed my eyes and checked the time on my phone: 4:45 pm. The park would be closing in fifteen minutes. Security should have been ushering people out by this point. Had they missed me? Either way, I had to make a move or be locked in for the night. My legs trembled below me as I rose to my feet. My back tensed forwards from the same sensation you get when you know someone's standing uncomfortably close behind you.

I turned towards the treeline across the river and caught a glimpse of something moving beyond the treeline. I breathed a sigh of relief as I realised it was just the branches of a tree swaying rhythmically. I rubbed my eyes. An early night was all I needed.

I started towards the exit, that feeling of dread following closely behind. The route that ran beside the cathedral and past the courtyard would be the quickest way out, since I had no intention of sticking around.

Walking through the gardens at this time gave it a liminal feeling, though I wasn't sure whether that was due to the lack of people or the way darkness turned familiar surroundings into a vague silhouette. It felt as if I were in a dream, walking through a mind's recreation of a distant memory. Were it not for the looming sense of being watched by unnatural eyes, I might have called it pleasant.

The exit wasn't far now, just down the steps would take me back to the flower beds and to the front gate. Descending, however, I did a double take at my surroundings, feeling bile begin to form in the pit of my stomach. In front of me was the same playground and bench that overlooked the river. Was I so disorientated that somehow, I'd looped back around? Something really felt off now.

I looked back into the treeline, the branches still swayed back and forth. But I could tell something was wrong. Before, the swaying branches resided behind the treeline; now I swore they were in front. Paralysis overtook me. I felt a hand grasp my rapidly beating heart from within my chest, making my body go numb as I gasped for breath.

The air was still. No other branch moved in the treeline. These swaying branches weren't moving in the wind. Rather, they were attached to something moving in on me. I looked further down into the trees, the hand around my heart tightened. Sweat streamed down my face as what resided behind the trees came into view.

What I saw across that river was no tree, but a humanoid shape wearing a cloak of unnatural darkness. Upon its head was a crown of dead branches that spanned into the treeline, blending in with them. If it had a face, it was shrouded in blackness. All I could make out was a pair of white orbs, staring back at me with a malevolent intensity. It was those eyes that held me in place with an invisible venom, paralysing me for it to do as it pleased. It took every ounce of my willpower to prise off the hand around my heart and let the blood flow back into my limbs, kick-starting my adrenaline.

Beyond that point is a blur to me, I only just remember how I sprinted back towards the exit one last time. Practically jumping the ruin walls and trampling the flower beds. I vaguely remember the security guard at the front gate that I shoved out of the way during my mad dash out, and the concerned glances and mutters from confused passersby as I leaped into my car and sped out of town and then away down the A14 at dangerous speeds.

I haven't been back since that night. But the stresses I

endured before were the least of my worries. Now, I barely sleep, and when I do my dreams are always the same. I'm back at the Abbey Gardens, paralysed as I watch those white eyes glide across the river towards me. I still don't know what it wanted with me that night. But despite how little I understood it, I've given it a name: The Abbey Watcher.

Great Livermere by Muriel Moore-Smith

Great Livermere is probably best known as the longtime home, if not residence, of M. R. James, medieval scholar and writer of ghost stories. His father was rector of the church and the family lived in the nearby rectory. Even though the village is only four miles northeast of the bustling market town of Bury St Edmunds, it has an isolated feeling, reminiscent of many of the bleak coastal settings favoured by James in his ghost stories. The church itself is thatched, white walled and has no coloured glass, which further emphasises this impression.

'In Heaven and Earth' is a re-imagining of an encounter from James' childhood which seeks to tie together some of the elements of his life: the plainness of his father's church in contrast to his later fascination with ornate medievalism, and his fascination with ghosts and horror despite his commitment to Anglicanism.

The childhood encounter was rendered by James himself in his final tale of the supernatural, *A Vignette*, and I have been inspired by his retelling of it in my own version. That he should have waited until the very end of his life to write about an event which spurred so much of his literary output is remarkable; this observation was very much in my mind as I wrote the last line.

In Heaven and Earth

'Why is the church so plain?' asks the boy. He had often wondered this as he sat and listened to his father's sermon.

The white walls, the clear glass windows, the unembellished wood, gave the entire place a puritanical aspect, as if it were trying to atone for some past sin. On the desk in front of him lies open a large book. He has learnt to pronounce the names on its pages - *Reims, Chartres, Notre-Dame* - but its coloured plates are what intrigue him: stained glass windows, each a distillation of the purest hue, like his mother's sapphire ring or the red jelly sweets cook makes with cochineal. Within their vaulted, bejewelled precincts, he could imagine a God capable of creating the blue sky above or the far-away moon and its bridesmaid stars. It is more difficult within the confines of his father's narrow church.

'The church may look plain to you, Monty, but as much care has gone into its construction as many of the great cathedrals you are reading about there.' His father sits down behind his desk and lights his pipe. It is important the boy realises that it is one's commitment to a cause which matters, not the scale of the achievement. 'You know, before I was sent to this parish, there was a man who gave his life to our church.'

The boy sits up. Death was history, the crooked lichen-covered tombstones in the churchyard, not something real and present and *alive.*

'You know that our roof is thatched? It is relatively unusual, even here in Suffolk, and people in the village think of it as a source of pride. One such man was Peter Gibbs. His family had thatched the church roof for generations. On the occasion of which we are speaking, it was Christmas Eve, and Peter was determined to have the roof finished in time for Christmas Day. But the day was bitterly cold and windy, such that everything was covered in ice and his hands were numb with cold. He was at the top of his ladder with the final bundle of thatch when a sudden gust of wind blew off the lake. His foot slipped and he fell thirty feet to the ground. They found his body in the Plantation on Christmas morning.'

'Our Plantation?' the boy asks, pointing to the large, wooded area running along the front of the garden.

'That is correct.' His father gets up from his desk and looks out of the window. 'So please remember that even the humblest church is built with faith and dedication.'

It is hard to forget a tale which occurred so close to where he lay that night. As he drifts into sleep, the boy thinks of the fallen man, of his bloody crawl along the gravel of the church path, of his effortful reaching to open the Plantation gate, of his cold, lonely expiration on the forest floor.

And in his dreams the man becomes able to do all things, things both of this world and of the other, so that when he hears a scuttling outside, the opening and closing of the locked front door, the steady thumping of a body up the stairs, he knows there is nothing he can do to stop it. He slides out of bed and puts his eye to the keyhole. Eye meets eye: one small and white, the other huge, bulbous, bloodshot, like something belonging to a great beast and yet there is such intent in the gaze.

He awakens with a start and sits up in bed. The hand he

passes over his forehead is wet with sweat. He goes to his bedroom window and looks out, but no one is there, and the house is still and silent. For surety's sake, he surveys the scene again and this time he fancies he sees something in the trees. Not movement exactly, more its exhalation, as if something on the ground had sent a quiver of air into the leaves and branches above. Yesterday he would not have seen it; today he can, although the new things he can sense are still faint impressions, as if seen through a sheer curtain, or heard through a closed door.

The next day, charged with delivering Father's forgotten prayer book to church in time for evensong, he is aware of the lawn moving, as if a rug were being straightened under his feet, and the edge of his vision is blurred. He blinks, tells himself it is a trick of the light – such things happen at dusk. But no, this phenomenon has been purposefully designed because, whilst his view of the rectory is hazy, everything in the Plantation is clear and bright, as things are in the cool, thin air of a mountaintop. He is being invited to look, to explore. Someone is waiting to welcome him in.

With his father's prayer book tucked under his arm, he walks along the wall towards the Plantation gate. Now he's attuned to it, the air hums like the reverberation of an echo and there is someone on the other side of the wall, matching him movement for movement as they hobble across the forest floor. He can sense their excitement at his impending arrival: the leaves skitter and fly under their feet. He can hear their breath.

He kneels in front of the gate and lays his father's prayer book beside him. On the other side of the wall there is a stilling, a gathering together, an intake of breath. The boy steadies himself, rests his hands on the wood, and lifts his eye to the keyhole. Another eye meets his, bloodied, bruised, the lower lid sagging and drooping like melted wax. The eye does not move or blink. Then – could it be so? – its corners lift imperceptibly.

Welcome. I have been waiting.

The latch clicks open. The gate moves under his hands.

He scrambles to his feet, grabs his father's prayer book, and runs as fast as he can. From inside the plantation comes a howl which warps and buckles the air. He has no idea of the rules which govern the dead, but he knows he will be safe in the church. He presses on, lungs burning. He is through the lych gate, into the graveyard, at the door. He twists the stiff handle, prays it does not stick, and arrives, panting for breath, at the back of the church.

'Everything all right, Monty?' his father asks from the altar where he is lighting the candles.

The boy merely holds up the prayer book. He hasn't the breath to reply.

'Ah, thank you,' says his father, indicating his book. 'Everything all right, old chap? You seem a bit perturbed.'

The boy nods and smiles. This evening, he will sit within the plain white walls of the church and listen to his father's sermon, whilst he calms himself and thinks how he can put into words what has just happened.

He has the feeling it will be a lifetime's work.

St Andrew's Church, Norton by Heather Rugg

This story begins within the graveyard of St Andrew's Church in Norton and follows the two protagonists as they leave the graveyard past the two oaks on Ashfield Road and ending in the home. St Andrews is a lovely, smaller medieval church with wonderfully large windows that fill the church with light. The church can be reached by turning off The Street into a small lane lined with a row of small cottages on the right. It is surrounded by fields that offer many popular walks for villagers and as the sun sets the church is bathed in sunshine. This church has a special connection for me and offers a peaceful tranquillity that gives space for being and reflection.

I was inspired to write this piece to capture the importance of meaningful connections with other people and the natural world. How the loneliness of being invisible and silenced can persist through time. When you can find a way to communicate with another person, this is a transformative experience that all sentient beings seek.

The Graveyard, the Girl, and the Gift

Yvaine stood silently beside an old gravestone that was chipped and tilted.

The carved names were long since lost to the weathering of time. She watched the young woman as she sat on the wooden bench that looked out onto the small rows of headstones that marked the graves of the local fallen heroes. Yvaine kept her distance, like a shadow just out of sight. She could see the young woman's face turned down towards the cold, hard earth, her black coat pulled tightly around her. She didn't want to disturb her. Her bright orange hat and scarf added a splash of colour to the autumnal scene.

Yvaine looked up at the greying sky. *Evening is approaching,* she thought. The long dark nights were a reminder of time moving on and another year becoming older. A mystical time that connects the spiritual and natural worlds. As a young woman, Yvaine had always liked this time of year: the rich abundance of colours, the reds, oranges, and gold of the leaves. Wrapping up in warm clothes, drinking mulled wine, sitting by the fireside and the excitement of Samhain, and the anticipation of Yule. She had loved the feel of the wind and rain on her face and laughed at the crunch of fallen leaves under her boots as she kicked her way playfully through them.

That was before.

Yvaine stopped herself from thinking more on this

painful subject and in the last dying light of dusk, she wistfully looked back towards the young woman. *She looks lonely, like me,* she thought.

'I will try and get a little closer,' she said aloud to no one and not really expecting a reply. After all, no one ever replies to the dead.

The young woman, Janneth, was unaware of her observer. She had grown up in the village of Norton. The church was her safe place to think. It had been a difficult year following the loss of her partner and she needed to sit here and clear her mind. She loved how the natural healing ambience around her soothed and swaddled her safely, like a child again.

As Janneth closed her eyes, she listened to the crows loudly cawing as they began to roost in the tall trees. She opened her eyes again to see the sun as it began to set behind the medieval church.

The last rays of light accentuated the colours of the leaves that still clung to the branches of the trees that lined the pathway up to the large wooden gate of the small stone narthex, the gathering space between the outside and the inner nave.

She drew in a deep breath.

'Beautiful, I love this time of year,' said Janneth, smiling as she kicked at a pile of leaves before her.

She let out a long sigh and stood up. Squinting in the light, Janneth thought she caught a very slight movement to her right, just beside an older gravestone. As Janneth leaned forward, she was startled to see a small figure emerge from behind the gravestone. It was a young girl, wearing a long grey coat, her long dark hair loosely flowing around her.

Straining her eyes in the dusky twilight, Janneth couldn't

make out any other features. She blinked and the figure was gone. She continued to look for a few moments more and saw nothing else and so turned to leave.

Yvaine had watched Janneth for only a few moments, but she noticed an openness in the young woman's demeanour, a kindness and empathy that comes from understanding life and the inevitability of death. She had overheard Janneth say she loved this mystical time of year too and hoping for a connection, she decided to take a chance and approach her.

'Can you see me? Can you hear me?' Yvaine said desperately, as she touched Janneth's cheek.

Janneth stopped suddenly and raised her hand to her face as she felt a tingle of cold on her left cheek. She swung around as she heard a humming around her.

'Is someone there?' Janneth asked in a barely audible whisper, her words stuck in her slightly fearful, dry throat. She looked up at the leaves rustling. I*t must have been the breeze through the trees,* she convinced herself.

'My name is Yvaine,' Yvaine said, standing very close to her.

Startled, Janneth turned around, causing Yvaine to take a step back.

This isn't working, I'm scaring her. How can I get her to trust me? Yvaine thought as she stared frantically around looking for inspiration at the leaves and stones that surrounded her. *Perhaps I can give her something*? Yvaine realised that the woman was about to leave and reached out, catching the young woman's arm.

Janneth felt a tug at her coat sleeve and a cold but gentle touch on her wrist.

'Please don't go. Not yet,' Yvaine pleaded.

As Yvaine looked down at her own hand around the

wrist of the young woman, she saw the ring her mother had given her. Taking it off her own finger, she pushed it into Janneth's hand.

Janneth looked down and instinctively closed her hand around the object. She drew her hand up and looked at the small gold ring with a star, initialled with a Y. She studied the ring, holding it up to the light and looking around, bewildered as to what had just happened.

Who has given me this ring?

'A gift! Thank you!' Janneth said, excited but perplexed. She tucked it into her pocket and hurriedly turned to make her way home.

I think she heard me, Yvaine thought hopefully, and followed behind Janneth as she began her journey home down the church lane, lined on the left with small cottages. She dropped back every time Janneth stopped and peeped over her shoulder.

'Hello? Is someone there?' Janneth asked.

The light had all but faded and the streetlamps were shaded by the branches of the two oaks that stood guard outside as Janneth safely reached her home.

That night, Janneth stirred from her sleep, not quite awake. Her bedroom felt still and silent as if time had stopped. The only noise she could hear was her heart pounding and her own gasps as she tried to catch her breath in the chilled air. As the light from the lamp post shone dimly through the window, she saw a small figure lying next to her. She could barely make out the figure but recognised her as the young woman from the graveyard.

'Is that you, Yvaine? Thank you for my gift,' Janneth said as she closed her eyes and fell back to sleep.

'Yes, it's me, Yvaine. I am just making sure you got home

safely,' Yvaine whispered, smiling, her voice filling up the silence like a gentle humming lullaby as she watched over Janneth sleeping.

Woolpit by Jayd Green

Sometime in the 12th century, two children were discovered in the village of Woolpit with green skin and an unknown language. Not knowing where the children were from or how they had got to the village, curiosity only increased when the children would only eat beans.

A number of theories have since tried to explain the siblings' sudden appearance: arsenic poisoning, abandonment in the woods, aliens, and their escape from a community that lived underground. The children's own explanation of where they were from told of a land of eternal twilight, with a great river dividing it from the much brighter neighbouring country.

This story follows the girl, apparently named Agnes, through her mysterious beginnings and eventual marriage.

Many thanks are due to Josh Read, historian and a local to Woolpit, who assisted in the gathering of historical and contemporary knowledge of the story. Those wishing to visit the sites of the story can still visit St Mary's Church on Rectory Lane in the village of Woolpit, or perhaps view the Woolpit village sign on Church Street that depicts the children's arrival. The wolf pits – as well as the wolves – are long gone.

Agnes Barre of St Martin's Land

They found us in the wolf pit. We could have been there a day or a year. To me, it had been an endless dusk. We could have once been the wolves they meant to trap. I remember the sounds of deer, trampling, eating vegetation, and the yelp of a fox. In the pit next to me was a small pile of bones, mice, or squirrels. I held them because they were the only thing that made me feel real. My brother was babbling, the language of a brook tumbling from his lips. I spoke back in the hush of a hedgerow. We understood each other perfectly.

When we were pulled roughly from the pit, into the glaring blaze of daylight, I held onto my brother because I thought they were taking him from me. I couldn't see, only shadows passed before me, agitated and looming, grabbing my arms and pulling me to my feet. They asked me things, which I now understand were, 'Who are you? Where have you come from? Where is your mother?'

To which my brother, young and confused, could only wail.

I tried to explain, but my mouth was still made of leaves and branches. It would remain this way for years: I would pick sticks and veins of plants from my teeth, my tongue furred and fat.

They walked us from the pit to the village, the people stopping their work and coming out to look at all the shouting. They were asked, 'Whose children are these?' but none could answer. As we walked, I stared at my hands, grown long and thin and green. I could rub the moss from my skin, but the stain remained.

'Does anyone in Woolpit claim these children?' the man continued to call out.

Eventually, I would tell them all I could remember. A dark and distant home, the smell of a wood fire, a ringing bell. The village people wrapped my head, which had bled.

When it healed, they took me and my brother to St Mary's, doused our heads in water and from then on, we had to visit the church regularly. Once the water hit my head, I would be called Agnes.

My brother died a few weeks later. The baptism meant he could be buried. While we read verses for my brother, I stared at the poppies on the pews. I opened my mouth, but no sound would come out. I think it was his heart, which broke with wanting for our home.

I told stories of a place I made up, called St Martin's Land, to explain how my brother and I had come to the village. I said things that didn't make sense, even if I remembered them. For a while people still felt pity for me, so they let it happen. There were rumours we had been poisoned, abandoned, and I felt eager to defend a family I didn't know I had. I decided they lived in my fictional place. In St Martin's Land, where my brother would still be alive.

Soon after my arrival in Woolpit, a boy I sat next to at church started to pinch my ribs and legs. He was very sneaky. He was not caught but I was called a sinner for yelping in church. After that, if someone annoyed me, or even if I liked them particularly well, I would pinch them. I thought that was what these people did. I tried my best to fit in, but I was a stranger to this village for many years, even as I lived within it. I was expected to keep quiet, even when I had something I desperately wanted to say, because it was rude to interrupt, especially if I was making a joke. I learned who could stomach my cheekiness and stuck to them.

When I was working as a housemaid for Richard, whom I would later marry, I was serving tea to a lady he was courting. She tutted at me for spilling the sugar. I let the thrill of the exasperation run through me, and reached forward and pinched her cheek, like you would a baby.

Richard laughed heartily, but the lady did not and left a few minutes later. Richard let me sit and finish the cake she had left on her plate. He was kinder to me in private, while many men were the opposite. I supposed that meant people thought he was weak or an upstart, like me. I married for selfish reasons: I was getting into a lot of trouble, and I thought I would be in less trouble if I were leashed by Richard.

On my wedding night, while my husband slept heavily because he was drunk and sated, I stayed awake and gazed out of the window. I heard a distant howl, or perhaps it was a bell, and ran out of the house in my wedding dress, forgetting my shoes. I tried to find the sound. I thought if only I could follow it, I could return to wherever I had come from.

Perhaps it was the wind I had heard, or the distant cry of a child. Branches twisted and snapped under my fast feet. When I got to the wolf pit, it had been filled in, like a grave.

Stowmarket by Molly Britton

Opened in 1936, the Regal Cinema in Stowmarket has almost a century of film history behind it. Located just off Stowmarket High Street, the cinema plays host to film screenings, live entertainment, and the 1936 Cafe.

I was raised to believe that ghosts are not monsters, or spirits, but echoes. These echoes are stronger at certain points, and I cannot think of a place more entrenched in these echoes than a cinema. I chose to set my piece in the Regal Cinema because of this.

Miss Morton, You're Needed on Set

'Miss Morten, you're needed on set.'

'Coming,' Rebecca replies, taking a shaky breath and rubbing at the trails of mascara that decorate her cheeks. She reaches for a brush with a trembling hand, shutting her swollen eyes to lightly dust her face with powder before opening them once more. She smiles, stands, and glides out of her dressing room, into the beaming studio lights.

It feels strange to enter The Regal without my grandparents. I cannot remember a time that I came here without them, our weekly trips to the cinema as much of a staple in our house as our weekly visits to church. It feels stranger still, after these last few years away from home in a city with three chain cinemas that all look the same, more so when the dust and grime from clearing out my grandparents' house clings to the knees of my jeans. I am hoping I don't bump into someone they knew, not wanting to hear the concerned questions, The 'Are you okay?' and 'How are you?' Not wanting to explain why I missed the funerals but made time for a movie. As it is, I manage to make it only as far as the cinema toilets before I bump into someone.

'Kay, sweetheart, is that you?' a woman asks me. She has short blonde hair and wears trainers that look older than I am. 'Are you okay? How are you?'

I'm not okay, I want to say to this familiar stranger, *I'm doing badly. I left my grandparents to go to uni and now they're gone and I'm all in pieces and nothing will ever be okay ever again.*

'Fine, thanks,' I reply hurriedly before ducking into a cubicle.

When the main door swings closed behind her, I leave the cubicle and stand at the mirror. I feel a soft brush of something against me, like fingertips touching my shoulder. I assume it's a breeze, though I can't say where from. It makes the hairs on the back of my neck stand to attention. I rinse my face with cool water, letting it drip from the end of my nose and into the sink. As my head is bowed, I register the lights flickering around me.

When I look back at my reflection, a woman stands behind me, dark-haired and blue-eyed, smiling slightly. When I turn, there is no one there.

'Reset, people,' the director calls. 'And Becky, it would be useful if you could actually know your lines this time.'

'It's Rebecca. And I knew them the first dozen times, Fred,' Rebecca replies. 'If you would let me rest, I'd be able to again.'

Behind her, the set dressers have replaced the broken wine glass with a new one, the overstuffed cushions have been plumped and adjusted on the hard prop couch, and her co-star had stood and begun to stretch, unconcerned about the continuity of his ever-changing mask, a combination of paint and bandages that renders the handsome man quite monstrous.

He chats with the Effects Manager, the two men conspiring together about ways to move his head to hide the seams of his face within his suit. Rebecca has watched the crew reset the scene almost twenty times now, and she fears she will watch it twenty more, but as the manager leaves, she knows that it is time for another attempt. She risks brushing a stray curl of dark hair behind her ear before Fred speaks once more.

'You can rest when you're dead, Becky. Places, everyone. Now.'

These have always been popular; the silver screen reruns. I should have expected a crowd as I return to the lobby. I try to remember these strangers from my childhood. I imagine someone breaking from the pack to shout at me for abandoning my grandparents and running off to uni. But no one does, and so when the tide of people ebbs, I join the flow into the smallest screen, taking a seat in the back row, a few spaces away from the aisle to avoid recognition from any stragglers.

Despite the surge outside, and the small, cosy nature of the screen, with only a few dozen seats, there are remarkably few people in the cinema, most of them apparently splitting off in the lobby to visit one of the two other screens, and I find that I get the back row mostly to myself by the time the lights begin to dim.

The film is just reaching its climax when I feel it again. The touch of fingertips on my shoulder. On screen, the leading lady screams as the monster grabs her, and simultaneously, I see what can only be called a ghost drifting into the empty seat next to me. I glance at the ghost from the corner of my eye. My arm on that side goes cold as she settles in the chair, her body below the knee disappearing into the plush seat, the rest of her floating just above it. I fix my gaze firmly on the screen, waiting for her to disappear.

She doesn't.

'I am telling you I will not do it,' Rebecca spits, tugging at where Fred's hand digs into the flesh of her wrist.

'And I am telling you that you will do what I say you will do,' Fred snaps back, clenching harder, compressing skin until it feels like bone. 'You are an overpriced prop, and if you won't do the scene as I say to do the scene, I will find another girl who will.'

'Fred, you're hurting me.' Rebecca struggles again, attempting to pull her arm from his grasp only for him to grab at the sleeve of her blue dress so that it rips slightly, the fabric spilling down her pale arm like ink on paper.

'You are under contract and for as long as you are, you will return to that set, and you will film the scene as I say. Do you understand?'

'Kay? Kay Morgan?' someone asks.

I look up and see a man I recognise as the neighbour who shared a back fence and a blackberry bush with my grandparents' house. The sound of the film almost drowns out the rasp of his voice, but I smile at him and nod, and point to the screen as if to ask that he let me watch the film in peace.

He sits down, leaving a seat and a ghost between the two of us. He leans across as if there is nothing there to loudly whisper to me. 'I haven't seen you since you were a teenager. Terrible shame about your grandparents. They were great friends. I thought I might see you at their funerals.'

'My grandparents decided I had enough funerals for a lifetime when I was a toddler,' I reply, a thin smile on my lips. The man whose name I cannot remember smiles sympathetically as if he understands.

'You come to see the picture?' he asks me, and I wonder how to answer in a way that isn't rude, given that he is speaking over the movie we have both come to see. I turn my face back to the flicker of the screen. He whispers something else to me, but I do not reply. I hear the squeak of the chair and when I look over next, he is gone and the ghost sits, quietly, watching the movie as if she too, is trying to memorise it.

Relieved at his retreat, and somehow more comfortable with the spectre that half-disappears into the seat beside me, the parts of her that touch the cushion turning to a fine mist on contact, I turn back to the screen. As I do, I feel two people drift into the seats on my other side. I risk a glance out of the corner of my eye and see two more spectres settled into the chairs, more abstract than the woman, their features less discernible, their forms more bent as they dissolve into the upholstery.

I fix my gaze forward, and clutch the armrests, not wanting to see any more.

'I want to go home. I want to see my little girl.'

'You will leave when I am done with you. Do you understand?'

Rebecca locks eyes with him, and something freezes in her when she glimpses the fury on his face. She nods and he releases her.

Rebecca retreats to her dressing room, clutching her wrist as she feels the familiar sting of tears.

'Boys, girls, ghouls, and undecided,' the manager begins, standing before the screen and talking into a microphone that whines as he brings it to his lips.

The woman floats on my right, the other ghosts settling back into their chairs on my left.

'We at the Regal want to thank you for coming here tonight to celebrate with us. It has been twenty years since this movie was released, starring Suffolk's own Rebecca

Morten, or Becky, as her friends called her. Her parents were very special to this community, and I am sure you have all heard of their recent passing.'

The crowd is sombre, respectful, remembering. I drop my head and feel the burn of a few sidelong glances in my direction. I ignore them, focusing on the memory of the relatives I remember, and the icy hot feeling of the spirits surrounding me before I feel a shift.

I look back up and watch as the ghost woman begins to drift forwards through the crowd, passing through people on her way to the stage. If anyone but me notices her, they don't show it, but I see a few people shudder as she dissolves around them, her vapour reforming on their other sides.

'Sadly, she never lived to see the film's premiere, but in watching it we remember her, and she lives on. I hope you will all join me in a round of applause in memory of her.'

On cue, a trickle of applause floats from the sparsely filled seats and towards the screen. At my side, two pairs of hands try to create the same noise, their wisps of palms gliding against each other silently.

The woman is standing before the screen now, facing the audience, the edges of her light blue dress and cape glowing even in the dim light. The echo of my mother looks at where I sit with my grandparents. Locking eyes with her, I drag my trembling hands from the armrests to meet in a quiet, hollow, sweaty clap. I pull them apart and bring them together again and again, joining in with the applause my grandparents cannot give.

Smiling, Rebecca bows.

Bentley Village by Jessica Spence

Between the villages of Bentley and Brantham in Suffolk is a short backroad. I was inspired by this road which I take regularly both driving as well as cycling. Learning about the history of the area and old abbey that once existed, I took an old legend and mixed them together to write this story. This story also blends with a recent incident I had with a pothole down that very road.

The Monk of Dodnash Priory

Another day over. That was the first thought that ran through Maria's mind as she left the pub. Another day, another long shift. She could hear the rattling of the keys in the midnight air as her boss locked up behind her before walking to his car beside her bike. Hands shifting over herself, she checked everything. Helmet, hi vis, light, drink, phone, emergency repair kit. *Tick, tick, tick*. She checked everything off her mental list before searching in her pocket for the set of keys. Creeping along the fence towards her bike she realised how dark it was tonight. Heavy clouds blocked out what little light the stars could give, the new moon lost in the sky.

Damn. She reached up to switch on her headlight. It was so dark she couldn't see her fingers as she fumbled the keys. *Clang, clang, schnict*. There. She finally got the lock off. Winding it around the frame of the bike she relocked it.

'Be careful out there.'

Maria got comfortable on her seat. Her boss sounded anxious, spooked even. Keys rattling as he toyed with them as he came to a stop beside her.

'You know me boss. Always am.'

Maria put on her warm smile, hoping it would calm her nerves. Though she had her doubts. Her boss had seemed off all night. As if something had rattled him to his core. *That's what you get for listening to old Tom*. Her boss had a habit of believing all the stories of their regular. Old Tom, the mad drunk of Tattingstone.

'Just be careful you know. That road is bad, Maria.'

Maria did one final check. Front light, back light. Check. Both were on and working. With a push, she was off.

God, she loved to cycle. Even on this cold dark night, there was still a thrill. She never saw the point in driving as she lived only a five-minute cycle ride away. Winding from the main roads to the wooded backroad that led to Brantham, the trees seemed to encircle her, turning the gloom into an abyss with only her light piercing through it. She was tempted to look into the old abbey grounds. At this time of year, the ground would soon be a sea of blue and purple flowers, perfect for a picture. But she knew the colours would be lost in the abyss. She was sure she saw a trace of white in the corner of her eye as she took the bend. *Must be a snowdrop*. She shook her head and focused on the road.

As she passed Bentley riding school, she could hear the snickering of the horses. They sounded like something had disturbed them. The road took a sudden plunge after the school. Steeper and bumpier as it cut into the valley. Maria reached for the brakes as she strained to see, wracking her memory for the road to feel where it narrowed for the bridge.

'Aaargh!' The bike flipped over. Light spun away as the world rolled. One second, she could see the edges of the bridge, the next the plunge of nothing. Ears ringing, teeth aching. She couldn't feel her limbs. Her breath stuttered as her brain tried to process what happened. Then all of a sudden, she was attacked by a thousand needles. Signals fired from everywhere. Her back, her legs, her hips. Firing on all cylinders to let her know where she had hit the ground. Cold seeped into her skin.

Her neck sent jolts of pain through her skull as she panned the black for a glimpse of light. There. A pale white bobbing to her left. *Wow, I must be rattled.* She felt like she was on a boat, her vision must be fuzzy. Maria swore the light was moving. With a series of groans, she clambered to her feet. Nothing felt broken, just sore. The blackness sparked as she felt everything spin.

Taking a few deep breaths, she began the slow march to the light of her bike. Or she was fairly sure it was her bike. Though her bike light had never bobbed before. Then the world seemed to sharpen in the gloom. Her light focused. There was her bike. But someone was playing with it.

The wheel spun as the peddle turned. A man, or she thought it was a man, hunched over it. Long brown coat, short curly hair, and hand to his face as if in thought. He seemed fascinated by her peddle.

'Hey, are you OK?' Maria was quite sure she hadn't hit anyone. Everything seemed muddied. The man didn't answer. His coat top fluttered. A shining cross glimmered underneath. *How odd.*

'Hey, Mister?' There was just the two of them and the spinning peddle. There was a weird glow about him. 'Sir, are you OK?' Maria slowly hunched forward. The man seemed to shake. Then he turned to face her.

Maria noticed the swinging cross first. Such a large thing. Before her eyes were consumed by the face. The man turned sharply, his head swinging on a pendulum. Left, centre, left, centre. Then his head fell off. Plop.

Maria froze, eyes wide with shock. She forgot about her step. Her foot fell into the pothole.

She screamed as she went down once more, rolling until she got her hands under her. Pain stabbed at her skull. On hands and knees, she crawled towards her bike. Chest heaving, heart pounding. The headless man was gone. Or was he a monk? There was just darkness. Only her bike lights pierced the abyss.

Maria didn't know how long she sat there waiting for the pounding drum that was her heart to settle. The darkness was her blanket. Soon the cold seeped in, stinging at her aches. With a groan, Maria picked up her bike. It was OK. She swung back on it. No point in pushing it.

With a push she rode over the old Abbey Bridge. But she didn't feel the thrill. Instead, she felt rattled to the bone. One thought consumed her. *Old man Tom ain't so mad after all.*

Alton Reservoir at Tattingstone by Sarah Waterson

The reservoir was constructed during the 1970s and 1980s, cutting the village of Tattingstone in two. Now known as Alton Water, there is a path that goes around the reservoir and people can walk, run, or cycle the path whilst enjoying a very peaceful and natural environment.

I remember taking walks around the reservoir with my dad when the reservoir was gradually filling up and seeing a tennis court being half submerged. It was very eerie and mysterious and there was a feeling of the land being very slowly immersed and absorbed.

Over the years, I have often walked around Alton Water and it is this memory that takes me back to that time when a village became physically divided and the landscape changed forever.

Being such a big expanse of water, there are several ways of getting to the reservoir, depending on where you are coming from. If travelling by car on the A14 towards Felixstowe, before getting to the Orwell Bridge, take Junction 56 and then stay on the A137. Eventually you will come to a crossroads (look for the Wheatsheaf pub on your left) where you turn left into Church Road (sign-posted to Tattingstone). Go past Tattingstone Church on your right and then turn left down School Road, which becomes Lemons Hill and then Lemons Bridge, which takes you over Alton Water. Once you reach the other side, turn right into a car park (there is also a car park just before the bridge on your left). From here, there is a path that takes you around the reservoir.

Going Home

It was the week before Christmas in the little village of Tattingstone. Lucy left her primary school on the last day of term. Already it was dark, and she hurried homewards among a gaggle of her classmates, their festive shrieks drowning out the country quietness. As the children arrived at familiar doorsteps, the group dwindled until eventually it was just Lucy, warm in her woolly hat, the one her mother had so lovingly knitted for her, walking on a frosted road that sparkled from the luminescence of fairy lights and flickering log fires behind cottage windows.

The night was cold and still. Woodsmoke curled fragrantly into the black sky stretching into an oceanic expanse of endless darkness, pale plumes that rose like the steam that pours from the funnels of a ship. Lucy stood in the snow, looking up. She imagined she saw trees, hedges, the shore of a lake or a sea in the swirling patterns. As she continued to gaze, there on the canvas of the night sky, an ethereal image slowly took shape.

It was a ghostly visage of a woman in a heavy coat, a woman with a pale indefinite face and large sorrowful eyes. The shadowy form seemed to hold Lucy in that moment. She was afraid, but the woman's gaze supplanted her fear with a depthless, all-embracing longing.

Lucy lifted her arms to the ethereal being. Slowly, the ghostly figure did the same, stretching as if to embrace the little girl on the sparkling village road. Then, as Lucy stared hard into the night sky, the ghost woman seemed to fall away, into the eternal sea of night, exploding into countless shards that burned brightly before being snuffed out by the darkness.

Lucy felt the sky darken, the stars going out. She stood still, dazed, shaking with cold and fear. Then at the end of the street, a shaft of light shone out. A front door opened. There was Lucy's mother, looking out for her, calling her name. The light and her mother's voice broke the spell. Lucy ran, slipping and sliding, and threw herself into her mother's arms.

Amy loved walking Basil her Beagle-cross, around the reservoir. She lived in the village of Tattingstone, which had been cleaved in two by the creation of a reservoir in the 1970s and '80s. She had only been a girl back then, but Amy remembered going on many walks with her father, gazing at the buildings slowly being submerged by the rising water. Over the decades, as Amy had evolved from girl to woman and her father had grown older and aged, they had continued to walk around the water together. After her father died, his ashes were scattered over his favourite piece of the shoreline.

Basil, nose-led, busied himself with the unfolding drama of scent. Amy watched him, wondering if he could detect her late father on some quantum level, so that Dad was both there and not there, leaving the dog sad and perplexed.

November had been very wet, and now, just a week before Christmas, it was rain and not snow that had been forecast for the yuletide holiday. The rain had swelled the reservoir and its rising waters rhythmically lapped at the foliage just a few feet away from the rugged path. Basil stopped and looked on intently. He was focused on Dad's favourite piece of shoreline, which was just a few metres away, partially obscured by mist.

'What is it boy? What can you see?'

Amy's breath clouded and hung in the air. The mist swirled and out of the agitation came the slow gait of a figure whose form seemed to Amy to be folded over by heartache and longing. Though still a few metres away, Amy could make out a tall, slender woman, her slow heavily booted feet, plodding to the water's edge.

Neither dog nor woman could move or utter a sound as they watched the dark-coated form enter the cold water. Slowly, raising her arms, she pointed and let out a long, desolate moan. It was as if she were reaching down into the depths, reaching down to someone below.

Around the reservoir, the trees and bushes were bejewelled with frost, white and sparkling in the moonlight. They reminded Lucy of the Christmas trees she had helped her parents to decorate over the years. She smiled at the memories. It was the week before Christmas, and it was at this time each year that their home had rustled with tinsel and excitement. She remembered the chaos of fairy lights hurriedly arranged by her little hands, of being lifted by her father to place the tatty old angel at the very top of the tree.

Lucy followed the path as it hugged the shoreline until she came to the place that was closest to her submerged home. The night was dark and cloudless, and the moon's luna beams seemed to plunge into the depths and halo her street under the watery sky.

Lucy kept looking until she saw the shapes of the cottages. Slowly, she walked into the reservoir, towards them, her boots filling with water, her large, heavy coat being tugged and pulled by the water, and by memories of all those Christmases from long ago. She hesitated, knee-deep in the rippling shallows, becoming aware of something. A woman and her dog, just a short distance away. Lucy continued her slow walk, down, down, down, into the water's depths, down towards what she knew would be the peace of her childhood street. Memories and what she could see merged like rivers and oceans; there was their Christmas tree, soft as seaweed, the moon's halo drawing her home deep beneath the waves.

Ahead of her, as the waters closed over, she saw a little girl, standing in the middle of the road, looking up. Lucy reached out to her. She felt the soft prickles of the child's woolly hat. The village embraced her in its darkness, where the snow fell and cocooned everyone in their cottages with fairy lights and burning fires.

The little girl stared up, and Lucy kept reaching until she *was* the little girl, and she heard her mother's voice, muted by the snow. Lucy turned towards the open front door, embraced by the light of their house. The freezing night sky submerged her as she ran towards her mother, towards home, towards the warmth of fairy lights under a watery sky.

Amy stood alone on the shoreline. It was here where the soil under her feet must still contain her father's ashes. She watched a misty form float and then disappear under the water, surrounded by a softly growing illumination, a ribbon of moonlight falling across the water. It was as if the moon itself was sinking into the black depths of the reservoir, going down to light the streets and the sunken cottages.

Silently acknowledging her father, Amy turned away

from the water and its mysteries, calling Basil to her side. She clipped on his lead, and both walked homewards, to their own warm and cosy cottage hearth.

Christchurch Mansion, Ipswich by Rose Dawn

Christchurch Mansion in Christchurch Park has been a museum since 1903. Before this, the Mansion was a family home from 1548 to 1895, but the site was originally home to the Priory of the Holy Trinity, which was destroyed during the reign of Henry VIII.

During its history, the Mansion was home to three different families: the Withypolls, the Devereuxs, and the focus of my story, the Fonnereaus. Emily Cordelia Fonnereau was the daughter of William Charles Fonnereau and Kate Georgina Cobbold, the sixth owners of the Mansion. Kate's marriage into the Fonnereau family started the Cobbold's association with Christchurch, as in 1895, Kate's nephew, Felix Thornley Cobbold, saved the Mansion from being demolished and gave it to the people of Ipswich. Emily's untitled poem about her desire to haunt the library is the only surviving information about her life.

Phoebe Fonnereau is the daughter of Reverend Claudius Fonnereau and Anne Bunbury, the third owners of the Mansion. Like Emily, little is known about Phoebe's life other than her portrait and her will. Phoebe lived longer than many members of the Fonnereau family, dying at the age of 82. In her will, she left money to provide bread for 400 Ipswich families.

I was inspired to write this story to highlight the lives of these two extraordinary women from the Mansion's history.

Phoebe's generosity and Emily's creativity solidifies their legacy as trailblazing women and serves as a wonderful reminder to always follow your own path.

The Library

'I think of a room that's very fair /
In dreams I'm often wandering there'

Emily Cordelia Fonnereau liked rainy days the most. On rainy days, she could sit in the library for as long as she pleased without anyone forcing her to go outside and play with her siblings. Emily was fourteen now and bored of their childish games. She would much rather spend her day in her favourite corner of the library. When she had awoken earlier that morning to the gentle patter of rain on her windowsill, she knew today would be a good day. Unfortunately, her mother had other ideas.

Kate Georgina Fonnereau was an esteemed member of the Ipswich Fine Art Club, or so she boasted. Often, on the days she could not go out and meet her fellow artists, she would disappear to the parlour to paint. But today, she decided her correspondence was more important. Kate was soon to exhibit at the Suffolk Fine Arts Association, a high accolade for the family, but for Emily, something that disturbed her reading time.

Kate settled herself at the grand oak writing desk in front of the library fireplace. Emily knew her mother had high wishes for her. She wanted Emily to make a name for herself in the art world, away from the clerical duties of her father. But Emily had her own ambitions. She dreamt of writing stories and seeing them living on these shelves amongst the names of her favourite authors. Yet she was apprehensive about picking up a pen to begin writing. She felt as if something or someone was holding her back.

She stroked the spines of the books on the shelf with her fingertips, then pulled one down and began reading.

Without looking up from her letter, Kate called to her daughter.

'Are you going to spend your entire day amongst the company of fictional beings, or are you going to make yourself useful and help to seal my letters?'

Emily snapped her book shut and trudged towards her mother. As she approached the desk, her eyes fell to the gold gilded mirror in the centre of the mantlepiece. She gazed upon her reflection, spotting a shadow drifting behind her, but when she turned around, there was nothing to be seen.

'Come now, Emily,' her mother scolded, passing Emily an envelope which she dutifully began to lick shut. As she moved the envelope away from her face, a cold breeze swept through the room from the direction of the staircase.

'One of those servants has left the shutters open again,' Kate muttered.

Still clutching the envelope, Emily watched as her mother picked up her pen and reached towards the ink pot. Before she could reach it, the pot flew across the desk and onto Kate's lap.

Emily jumped. Her mother shrieked as the sticky ink stained her fingertips, spreading over the table and dripping into the expensive lace of her dress. She rose from her chair and stormed out of the library. Emily watched her go, peering down through the internal window.

As her mother hurried away down the stairs, Emily thought the eyes of the family portraits that crowded the staircase walls appeared to follow her. Rubbing her own eyes in disbelief, she looked back at the portraits, but now they resembled their normal selves. All except one. The portrait of the shepherdess above the staircase whose eyes remained fixed on Emily's.

Emily knew this girl was a distant relative, but she often daydreamed in her father's family lectures, so she was unsure of her relative's name. As she continued to stare at the portrait, she heard a crash in the library. She turned quickly to see the glass doors of her father's locked bookcase swing open. This was the one bookcase Emily had never explored. She was uninterested in the numerous volumes of *Justice of the Peace,* but she knew this was where the family records were kept.

Slowly, she approached her father's book ladder beside the open cabinet. She climbed the ladder, and glanced at the titles on the shelves, spotting *Duties of Men* and *Paradise Lost* before locating the family records, tucked in the corner of the top shelf. She reached for the volume, but it just evaded her grasp. A low rumble of thunder echoed outside. Emily leaned further towards the shelf, pushing herself up on tiptoes as she wobbled on the ladder. A flash of lightning shone through the stained-glass window. The wheels of the ladder inched forwards, hitting the bookcase with a thud. The book fell into Emily's hand, opening on an entry that read:

Phoebe Fonnereau
1747 – 1829
Died at Christchurch in her 82nd year
Never married.

Emily clutched the book to her chest and looked back towards the pile of papers spread over her mother's desk. The room was once again illuminated by a flash of lighting and suddenly, the disused clock in the centre of the table began to chime.

Emily stepped down from the ladder. She approached the chiming clock, her eyes returning to the portrait of the shepherdess.

'*Phoebe*?'

Phoebe watched her through the open shutters. Emily heard the drawer creak open next to her mother's seat. There, she noticed a spare pot of ink. Emily looked back at Phoebe.

'Are you guiding me to *write*?'

Emily felt the chill of the breeze again, blowing the spare papers towards her. Slowly, she picked up her mother's pen, seated herself on the woven bench and began to write.

'If 'ere my ghost walk mortal ground /
I think it will be in this library found'

The Woolpack, Ipswich by Alec Taylor

The Woolpack in Ipswich is one of the oldest and most historic pubs in the town. There are indisputable records from the seventeenth century and reports dating a pub at the site to as early as the 1400s. Originally sited just outside one of the main town tollgates, the pub has had a colourful history, replete with priests in hiding, smugglers, and murderers. Needless to say, a pub of this stature has its quota of ghosts. The best-known Woolpack spook is British Admiral Edward Vernon (1684-1757), famed for his victory in the Battle of Jenkin's Ear. Vernon served as Ipswich's MP and lived on the estate that is now Orwell Park School. He was known as Admiral Grog on account of his penchant for wearing a coat of a coarse silk fabric called grogram. After Vernon watered down the navy rum ration in an effort to reduce drunkenness, *grog* became assimilated into the English vernacular. This story focuses on Admiral Grog and gives a shout-out to some of the other apparitions reported at the Woolpack over the years.

Admiral Grog

'Evening Donna, what's everybody having?'

'You made it then, Ryan.'

'Of course. I wouldn't want to miss a chance of getting one over on Dave. Hmm, they've done an excellent job of decorating the old place. Very tasteful.'

'Still haven't got rid of that black mark over the fireplace, though. I'll have double Gosling's 151 rum please, Ryan, neat. Better get a shift on. The quiz starts in ten. Bar, Ryan, *vite*.'

Gosling's 151 rum was expensive. Newly single Donna knew it. She fancied Ryan and had an inkling that the feeling was mutual.

'I'm just going to get some fresh air, boys.'

Donna slipped out of Woolpack pub. Glancing up at the distinguished red brick hostelry, she awed at the five-hundred years it had stood guarding the road into Ipswich. In the beer garden, she was alone. She would only normally put herself through the physical wrench of entering the astral plane when there was money to be made at poker or the casino. But Donna could not countenance coming second to her ex-boyfriend, Dave. Also, she'd heard dishy Ryan was currently writing ghost stories. If she could provide Ryan with first-hand accounts of Admiral Grog and the other Woolpack spooks, this would really impress him.

Each breath slower, deeper than the last. Serene, motionless, she allowed the migration to begin. Hot plasma searing her skin. Electricity paralysing every muscle. A thousand colours swirling in an accelerating vortex. Screaming, thundering, deafening noise. Her tongue burning with acid. The rancid smell of death. Tumbling backwards out of the mortal realm and into the astral plane.

A warm iridescent ether enveloped her body as she arrived. The astral plane, the spirit world, the synthesis of time and space. Donna drifted back into the bar, red brick walls flowing through her body with only the merest hint of resistance. She could see Dave talking behind his hand to a lady friend, whilst the pair watched Ryan at the bar.

Donna's gossamer body hummed and purred as she propelled herself back in time with superlative skill. Just as she had hoped, the quizmaster was having a read-through thirty minutes before the quiz.

Ah, Irish geography, I always mix up the Bann with the Foyle. Ryan isn't going to like him calling Derry, Londonderry.

Donna memorised the celebrity picture round and the few other answers she did not already know. Now to look for Grog.

Donna had travelled back hundreds of years before, for her own amusement. There was no chronometer to guide her progress, only clues. Uniforms and blackouts signposted World War Two. More uniforms denoted the Great War. Random scenes of well-dressed people, singing around the piano and sitting by a log fire, flashed by. The Woolpack seemed to be always full. Donna slowed to a halt, she needed to know the date. It was dark, save for red logs spluttering sparks and yellow flares. Donna could just make out the wall clock showing ten past twelve. She needed to find something with a date, a newspaper, maybe.

A modest light illuminated the room. Somebody was on the plane with her. Hands cupped her eyes for a moment, nubbly grogram silk skittered across her cheeks.

'Stop searching, I'm here. I followed you from 2024.'

'Old Grog?'

'Admiral Edward Vernon MP to you, young lady.'

Donna looked at Grog, dashing in his blue frock coat and tri-cornered hat. There was something familiar about him.

'I was expecting you to be older.'

'When one chooses to spend eternity walking the astral plane, one gets to assume any bodily form that one might encounter. Including a younger self. Sometimes I even manifest as erstwhile landlord George.'

'Why's that? Wasn't George murdered?'

'Murdered for hiding a mad priest. The sight of George sends him scurrying back to his priest hole.'

'So, I take it the priest is the ghostly monk?'

'The very same. Hunted to his death. Driven so insane he climbs the walls like a spider.'

'What about the drowned sailor?'

'Fred? Let's find him.'

Grog took Donna's arm and the pair fluxed into the 1730s.

'There he is, guzzling a surfeit of ale. A few years hence we should meet his spirit.'

Sure enough, on a frosty winter night in 1733, Fred dragged his filthy wet carcass through the door. If it were possible to be simultaneously both alive and dead, then this was Fred. He stumbled and slid across the beer-soaked sawdust as Grog's long leather boot connected with his backside.

'Begone from my realm, you fetid swillbowl.'

Fred stumbled through the wall.

'Tell your friends to watch out for Fred. He has taken many disguises over the centuries to avoid my boot. He loves this place and will never leave.'

'Changing the subject, did you actually see Jenkin's ear?'

'Ah, yes, The Battle of Jenkin's Ear. Pickled in Jamaican rum it was. That drunken rakefire Fred would have eaten it and drunk the liquor, given his chance.'

'You're famous for watering down rum, yet you dwell in a pub?'

'I once owned the Orwell estate, but I cannot go back. There's too much sadness there for me to bear. I lost my darling Sarah and my three sons, only James reaching manhood. Not one of them gifted to join me on the astral plane. So, I must abide here in the Woolpack's eternal company.'

Grog took Donna's hand.

'You know, you remind me so much of my darling Sarah.'

Alarm bells sounded for Donna. The past was nice for a visit, but she did not want to stay. She jolted backwards. A half-gallon bombard crashed above the fireplace. A grey headless creature scuttled down the wall and through the floor.

'Damn you, Priest.'

Donna sped back towards the present before Grog could join her. She rejoined her body in the beer garden. That which was taken from her as she had departed the mortal realm was returned in an exquisite rush of pleasure. That fabulous rum beckoning, she rejoined Ryan as the quiz started.

'What was the name of the first ghost to visit Scrooge in *A Christmas Carol*?'

A crash of breaking glass stopped the quiz. Donna looked at the picture that had fallen from the wall. *Edward Vernon and family, Orwell Estate 1739.* Good grief, she was Sarah and old Grog ... Ryan?!

'Are you OK, Donna? You look like you've just seen a ...'

'Have you put water in this rum?'

Ipswich Waterfront by Chris Odogwu

My story was inspired by the paradox of water – it's both useful and potentially harmful. The sea at the Waterfront captures this idea. As an international student who is new to Suffolk, the Waterfront is one of the areas I'm most familiar with, so it was a great location choice for setting the story. I wanted the readers, especially those who haven't been to the Waterfront, to get a glimpse of the beautiful area against the backdrop of an eerie ghost story.

Withered Roses

I like the feel of the sea breeze caressing my skin as I sit on the patio of the Waterfront Building in Ipswich, savouring the magnificent view of the blue and white skies above the water and the sailboats.

This is a routine for me whenever I'm on the Suffolk campus, so it's not unusual that I'm here. What's unusual is that I'm alone. There's no one sitting around me, walking in and out of the building, or strolling on the road. I don't remember how I got my coffee. All I know is that it's in front of me, its steam rising from the cup into my nostrils. I don't think much of it; it's probably one of those days when I feel forgetful.

I sip my coffee slowly, mindful of its hotness and look around, admiring the scenery. As I return to watching the boats, I see a young woman in a white dress standing some metres away, her back facing me. My heart skips. She wasn't there a second ago, I swear. She knows my gaze is on her. She turns towards me, revealing the right side of her face.

'Follow me,' I hear a feminine voice say. I don't see the woman's lips move, but I'm convinced the voice is hers.

I don't want to follow her, but I get to my feet and walk in her direction like a zombie. As I get closer, she turns and begins to walk.

The intensity of the wind increases, her long hair flying as she walks towards the water. I open my mouth in astonishment as she dips her foot in the water. I'm afraid that she will fall over but she doesn't. She's walking in the water, her body sinking with each step she takes until she's submerged.

I open my eyes. I'm in bed in the dark. The familiar vanilla fragrance tells me that I'm in my room. It was a dream. I heave a sigh, but my relief is short-lived. I have a hunch that the woman from the dream is in my room, too.

I reach for the light switch beside my bed. She isn't here. I turn to lie on my right side only to see my laptop on the floor. I always keep my laptop on my desk. How did it get there?

I recall the events from last night. I was exhausted upon getting home after an intense workout session at the gym, so I jumped into my bed for the night. I don't remember seeing the laptop on the floor when I returned home. Even if it was on the floor, I don't remember putting it there.

I get off my bed to pick up the laptop. As I move closer to it, I notice the Google Doc page on its screen with the words 'IT WASN'T A SUICIDE' boldly written in Times New Roman font. I stay still, staring at the words, trying to understand what they mean and how they got there. I'm certain I didn't write those words. Who wrote them, then? My head starts to ache from so much pondering. I hope this is another dream.

I hear my neighbour's voice from outside, it's not a dream after all. I'm not about to go crazy over this supposed mystery. I decide that it's all a prank. That's the only logical explanation.

I'm seated in class on the third floor of the Waterfront Building. At least twenty of my classmates are in the room.

I can hear the voice of our Philosophy lecturer, Dr Daisy, who is standing in front of the class teaching, but my mind is preoccupied with the events of this morning. I see a hand drop a piece of paper on my desk. It's reading material for the class. I pick it up: 'A Valentine's Day Drowning,' the article title reads.

On February 14, 2001, two young lovebirds – Harry and Viola – had booked a sailboat on the Waterfront dock to celebrate Valentine's Day. Some passers-by reported seeing them getting on the boat at dusk, and others reported seeing them sailing on the boat later at night. Around 9pm, Harry alerted the sailor that Viola had jumped into the water. They called 999 and the coastguard arrived at the scene. After searching the waters, they found Viola's lifeless body. Her death was classified as a suicide. There was no evidence to prove otherwise.

I take a closer look at the black-and-white photograph of Viola in the article. She looks like the lady in my dream. She's wearing the same white dress and her hair is flying in the air, just like it was in my dream. I remember the inscription on my laptop. My father's name is Harry. Is Viola trying to tell me something?

I feel goosebumps on my body, a rush of cold waves swirling around my head – the hairs on my arms rising. I clench my fingers on the paper, close my eyes, and begin to take deep breaths.

I feel a pat on my shoulder. I open my eyes and as I turn, I see Viola's face right before mine.

'Your father pushed me into the water,' she whispers.

St Mary-le-Tower Church, Ipswich by Daniel Snowling

Nestled in the heart of Ipswich, set back from Crown Street in the town centre sits *St Mary-le-Tower* Church. Despite being rebuilt three times since its beginnings in the late Saxon era, St Mary-le-Tower is still seen as a landmark for cultural and religious heritage in Ipswich. When I first visited the church, I couldn't help but appreciate the contrasting brickwork of the tower and the way the building seemed to tell its own story through its architecture. Once inside, I was taken in by the ornate wooden sculptures that hid around the foyer, but the main draw for me was the organ. The old, dark metal pipes added a character to the building, one of mystery and a sense of some ancient secrets housed inside them, and the music once played through them. When imagining the sounds that these pipes would make, I knew then it was here that I would set my story.

When starting the *Suffolk Haunts* project, I became interested in the relationship between the belief and non-belief of ghosts and the supernatural, and through my writing, I wanted to create a sense of doubt and unease for the audience. Early versions of this work dealt with trying to communicate a character's unfiltered thoughts; this then evolved into the piece you are about to read. I chose to focus on a singular, hard-to-rationalise moment of distress for the main character, and through this experience explore who they are and how the event is connected to them.

When the Music Stops

The organ is blaring but there's no one playing it. No one's sitting in front of it or moving the ivory keys. It's beautiful, the music, but dark, and it won't stop. It's like nothing I've heard before, or maybe I have, but a long time ago. Some obscure nocturne, Fauré or Chopin perhaps … There can't be something wrong with the thing, can there? Or is it a cruel prank, perhaps? Or am I imagining the music and I've lost my mind completely? I'm not sure what's more comforting … But it's definitely playing, and I can't get out.

For half an hour I've been pressed up against the heavy church door, and for an hour before that, I kept pushing and pulling at the heavy iron handles, again and again, but they didn't budge. I have slammed my hands on the windows, hoping someone outside would help me, but any passers-by just kept walking, as if they could hear no sound at all.

I don't dare move now. If I just crouch here, on the floor, my back resting against the door, and my eyes on the black metal pipe organ … I will be OK. Nothing bad will happen. It hasn't happened yet. Whatever it is that is making the music will just keep ignoring me. Whatever *it* is. Whatever is playing. So long as it keeps playing, so long as the music continues perhaps, I'll be OK. God, please don't let the music stop. Don't let the sculpted creatures on the pews or the gilded statues turn to look at me.

I should have gone home when Tim did. But how could

I have known this would happen? How could I have known that as soon as I finished blowing out the candles, getting ready to leave, that the organ would start breathing, start playing all by itself? I should have caught the earlier bus back, no matter how much I hate being home, how empty it feels there. I shouldn't have stayed late to work more on my music, I know it all already, I know it backwards.

I have stood here for so long, looking straight at it, seeing nothing at all, and all this time I've been waiting for someone to appear from under the organ, to walk out from the dark wooden booth with a smile on their face and say it was them all along.

When the music began, it made me think of Dad. He used to play the piano in an orchestra and taught me to play, too. He performed to crowds every night and I would always watch how his playing affected people, seeing the life in their eyes brighten …

I play for no one, or rather, no one really listens. As a church organist I'm shut away in the little box that my eyes are glued to, whether it's a wedding, a funeral, a mass … I'm the part of the church to never really be looked at. Dad used to say while we played together that our music was something we could share and that no one would be able to hear except for us. I never really knew what he meant by that and I'm still not sure. But it's too late to ask him now, Dad is buried in the cemetery here. Now it's just me that can hear the music. I need to pull myself together. I'm just being stupid, pathetic … There's nothing here! I can't see anything, so it doesn't exist. This whole moment doesn't exist, the music, the playing, the doors, and how I feel, all nothing. Take me up to the tallest building or better yet, the top of a wooden bridge, and I'll be afraid. I see where I can fall, I know where to run from. So why? Why when I see nothing, does my stomach knot? Why are my nails digging into my palms, and why are my veins as cold as the tiled floor I lie on?

Then the music stops. Like the graves outside, it falls silent. As silent as it was just before it started playing at me. To me. For me?

I rally myself to my feet, my arms tucked closely to my chest. I look to the organ, and then around the open spaces and empty pews. I'm incredibly aware of the space above me. Of the dark rafters. The hidden corners behind the pillars. The shadows in the wings.

All is quiet now, except for rain tapping against the stained-glass windows. I hear footsteps echo through the hall and feel a chill run through me. I'm sure I did ... Or was it me imagining things?

I can't control my breathing anymore, my chest is tightening, as if something I should run from is getting closer to me. I go to turn to the door, to try just one more time to heave it open, but as I turn, I notice a single candle glimmering meekly in the corner of the foyer. Kindled once again. I put all the candles out earlier ... I know I did, so how is it lit? I must have missed one, I must have made a mistake.

The fire, dancing softly on the wick, doesn't panic me. The faintest feeling of calm warms me and I briefly forget about where I am, trapped between the locked door, the black-beamed ceiling, and the now sleeping organ.

I forget about the fright. I forget about the music. All I can think of is that little candle, waving at me, and from that flame my body relaxes. I let go of the door handle and after a long resounding thud the church is silent once again.

Now it's just me, I think I miss the music.

The large door next to me eases open, sending a gentle inhale through the church, slinking past me and across the stone walls and dark terracotta-coloured tile floor. I swear I hear the organ sigh.

I realise I can leave. I can be free from this place and forget about the organ, the music, and the candle that is now flameless, a sliver of silver smoke swaying upwards from its wick. I should go home; I'm not dreading it now. But I stay for a few more minutes, in the quiet, alone. Except, I don't feel alone, and for the first time since Dad died, I feel calm.

I should visit him soon. I miss him, but I'm ready to talk to him again.

The River Orwell by Roy Haddock

If you stand at a place called the Strand locally on the B1456 and look up to your left, you will see the concrete arch of the mighty Orwell Bridge spanning the river. To the right, past the wading birds on the mud flats, the river winds its way past Pin Mill.

At night, the beauty of the place changes to a dark eerie silence. The darkness almost becomes an entity in itself. This is a story of the bridge, the river, and its darkness. The darkness is many things, it can creep into all of us.

Nightmare on the Orwell

Jan had reached the yacht late. Her train had been delayed and now, sailing out of port, she couldn't see the Harwich harbour master. She had worked for the Barkers before. They never went far, but never sailed back, so normally easy money for her. With the new boat being ten feet longer, she couldn't sail back to Ipswich, not on her own. Even with its diesel engine, it would not be easy. Her biggest fear was arriving after dark, and now that was inevitable. To moor anything this large in daylight was frightening enough.

Chugging up the estuary, she looked on as the light faded and darkness set in. The full moon shimmered on the water, set against the cloudless sky. Stars twinkled against black velvet.

Arriving at Pin Mill, Jan saw the lights emanating from the houses along the riverbanks. Warm and inviting, their reflections glimmered like candles in a church. Everything was still. Only the gentle ripple and the engine's *chug-chug* broke the silence.

The clear night brought a chill to the air. Jan pulled her fleece zip higher, occasionally warming her hands in its soft pockets. Peering through the mist of her breath, she could see the red and green buoys marking the channel. She had travelled this stretch so many times, and she was always pleased to get here.

Not long now.

As she approached the bend of the river, the silhouette of the Orwell bridge came into view. The never-ending headlights of the vehicles crossing its back under the moonlight made it almost magical. Jan stared at the bridge and saw a tiny figure which seemed to move.

What's that? Disappearing and then reappearing further along?

The passing headlights illuminated the figure's new position.

Reducing speed, Jan fumbled for a pair of binoculars in the navigation box.

They're in here somewhere ... I saw them earlier.

Finding the small pair, she examined the lenses using her phone's light. They would do. Gazing up at the bridge, she struggled initially to locate her target. Slowly, as the yacht got closer, it came into focus.

It's a person. What are they doing? Jan looked harder. *They're on the edge. Oh, God, are they going to jump?*

She grabbed her phone from her pocket. Without removing her gaze from the figure on the bridge, she dialled 999. Nothing. She looked down. The screen became blank. Jan felt for the radio near the helm, switching it to the emergency channel.

'Mayday! Mayday!'

There was no reply. The radio was dead. *How could that be?* She had checked both before leaving.

The yacht continued slowly, getting closer and closer. Jan felt her anxiety rising. Although cold, she started to sweat.

Why is no one stopping? Why does nobody help?

Uncontrollably, she started shouting into the night.

'Help! Help!'

There was no one to hear her. The bridge loomed closer. Suddenly, simultaneously, the phone and radio sprang into life. Frantically, Jan dialled again.

'Emergency,' came a voice. 'Which service do you require?'

'Police, police! Someone is going to jump.'

The yacht edged under the bridge. She could no longer see the figure.

'Can you hear me? I said they're going to jump!'

THUD.

The bow of the yacht dipped to the port side. A wall of water rose and as the yacht pitched from side to side, it washed over the deck. Jan grabbed the wheel and held tight until it righted and steadied. Instinctively, she stopped the engine. She was on her knees and briefly felt disoriented. Her phone slipped from her hand and landed face up on the deck. The yacht veered. A whirlpool pulled it around as it drifted beneath the bridge. She regained her balance. Slowly, she stood and brushed herself down, feeling to see that she was OK. Muffled voices broke the silence. Jan gazed about her, confused. Then she noticed the lit screen. She bent down and grabbed the phone.

'Miss, are you there?'

'They've jumped, hit the boat. I'm trying to find them!'

She slipped down the boat's side, shining her phone torch to light up the deck. She saw no one. Leaning over the bow, Jan scanned the moonlit water from left to right. Nothing.

As she turned, a figure appeared. With a sudden shock, she dropped the phone.

The presence stood some six feet tall, shimmering, almost translucent, although solid. Its form resembled that of a human. Around its edges, there was a dim glow of an outline. It had no features apart from a large gaping mouth and two pale green eyes.

Jan stumbled backwards, falling against the safety wires of the deck. Trying to retreat, she pushed herself back, but she had no escape. Fear was now controlling her actions.

The figure shimmered. Its movement seemed to replicate breathing. Weed hung from its limbs. Then it seemed to gasp.

'*Help me …*'

Jan covered her ears. The reek of rotting weed and mud permeated the air. The figure turned, raised an arm, and pointed to the river. '*Help me*,' it hissed again.

Jan was frozen. Her limbs would not move, and now the presence felt closer. Although it wasn't breathing, she could somehow feel its breath. Reeling backwards to avoid contact, she could smell the stench intensifying. She closed her eyes and turned away. Her skin was clammy and she felt sick, as if she had been spun around like a child on a roundabout.

'What do you want?' she screamed.

'HELP ME …' it hissed into her ear.

Then there was silence.

Jan turned her head gingerly and opened her eyes. There was nothing there.

Crying and shaking, she began to move up the boat. With no light other than the moon, she stumbled to the helm, started the engine, and pushed the throttle to full. As she passed under the bridge, she felt a cool breeze at her neck, causing her to turn. Something appeared over the water in the distance. Two pale green eyes.

Felixstowe Landguard Fort by Elise McManus

This ghost story is based on stories of the ghosts at Felixstowe's Landguard Fort, combining legends of ghosts from multiple time periods. I chose this not only due to personal connection, as I currently live in Felixstowe, but for the opportunity this provided to explore friendship between the ghosts and to write a story that blends a ghost story with comedy.

The Ghost Tour

What a glorious night to be dead.

Standing on Landguard Fort's bastion, Captain Kelsey repeated the same nightly round he had undertaken for over eighty years, three in the land of the living, and seventy-seven in the world of the dead. As the storm raged on, he paused and stared out across the water. It was the same view as it had been in 1941: the rough waves, the blinding light of cranes by the dockside. Beneath the rain, he could hear the metallic clank of containers being lifted, distant shouts carried by the wind. He closed his eyes.

He had realised there were many perks to being a ghost. At first, his invisibility was distressing, but for a man like him, a man who preferred to observe quietly, it soon had its merits.

Meticulous in life about his appearance, Kelsey had spent hours trimming his moustache and polishing his boots. Now, his uniform materialised onto his body. Often, he wondered how many ladies would wish they could die for the convenience of pristine ghostly dresses. The rain rolled from his shoulders. His grey hair remained dry.

'Kelsey! Kelsey, get down from there! You'll be late!'

Kelsey groaned. There it was – the drawback. One had to spend the afterlife with other ghosts.

He looked down to see Captain Russell staring up at him, shielding his eyes from the rain. Whilst Russell had been dead a good sixty years longer than Kelsey, he still had not entirely given up on human habits. Kelsey wished he disliked him. He was not the kind of soldier that the decorated, respected Captain Kelsey wished to associate with. He was crass and arrogant and wore his red uniform in disarray. He had died drinking gin taken from the loaded hold of a smuggler's ship. Yet for all his faults, Kelsey could not hate him.

'Our adoring public awaits!' said Russell.

'Doesn't it feel cheap to you? Quite degrading?' Kelsey replied.

Russell snorted. 'I'm not letting you sit another one out. Come along, let's go see if Williams is up for it.'

Reluctantly, Kelsey followed, rolling his eyes at Russell's swaggering walk. Williams was never up for it, but he could not help but admire Russell always asking.

'What do I do?' Kelsey asked.

'Just be yourself,' said Russell.

Ghost tours had become so popular that the fort hosted several a month. They were even more popular when Russell, egged on by a young ghost, had started playing tricks on the guests, letting himself be noticed, even seen. His newfound celebrity status had made him perfectly obnoxious to deal with.

They crossed the fort and headed for the Chapel Bastion. They did not open the door. Whilst it was no longer locked, they knew Williams well enough to know he would not take kindly to them barging in. They had never seen him in the light, in fact. All their conversations went through the stone wall.

'Hello, old chap,' said Kelsey. 'Ghost tour tonight, if you fancy it.'

Williams let out a groan. He had been locked away in the small room almost three-hundred years ago to hide the plague that eventually claimed his life.

'No ... No, thank you,' he said eventually, 'bad night. Bad night tonight.'

'We understand,' said Russell. He looked to Kelsey and whispered, 'I suppose you get used to hiding.'

'Yes,' replied Kelsey, quietly.

There was no time to linger. The noise of the overnight ghost tour was approaching. They watched the group, huddled in layers of waterproof coats, carrying strange-looking radio devices and remotes. Russell laughed at the sight of it. The guide gave a surprisingly correct account of their lives, one that even Kelsey could not sniff at.

Russell brushed his lapels. As one ghost hunter laid down the radio, emitting loud static that made Kelsey wince, Russell experimented with tapping the radio, shouting curses and wafting his hands in front of it. Technology delighted him.

'Give it a go,' said Russell. 'They can hear us on it, you know, or so they say.'

Kelsey sighed and stomped over to the radio.

'Hello,' he said to it. It crackled in response.

'I think it just said "hell"!' cried one ghosthunter in awed tones.

Kelsey rolled his eyes.

'Come on!' said Russell, bounding after the tour as they walked up to the bastion. 'Look, they're going to your round!'

Kelsey was almost offended at the short amount of time the ghost hunters spent on the bastion. After moments of polite hesitation, they headed right for the gift shop, part of the fort that Kelsey seldom explored. There were rows of brightly coloured postcards and shelves of Airfix model planes. He longed to reach out and tuck a magnet or pencil into his jacket, but restrained himself, knowing that it would only clatter to the floor.

'The grand finale,' said Russell, approaching the model planes. He cracked his knuckles.

Kelsey sighed and looked away. He caught a flash of glass and saw that behind the till was a mirror. Instinctively, he backed away. It had been years since he last saw his reflection, not since … Curiosity weighed equally with his nervousness. He snuck away to look at himself.

Oh … Is that all? He looked precisely how he did the day he died, bleeding forehead and all. He raised a hand to the ghostly blood. It seemed hardly threatening, now he knew what it looked like.

Suddenly, there was a scream. A woman was pointing directly at the mirror, and Kelsey realised his ghostly reflection was not as invisible as he thought.

As heads snapped towards the mirror, Kelsey flew back, hitting the till. As he lunged forward to try and catch it, it bounced onto the floor, spilling loose change. Losing his footing, Kelsey reached for a stand of postcards, managing to pull it down to the floor with him. As coins and paper scattered across the floor, Russell gave the shelf of Airfix planes a mighty shove, and two bounced to the floor. The ghost hunters screamed both in horror and delight, torn between running to investigate the till or the planes.

Russell gave a hearty laugh. He tossed the postcards aside and pulled Kelsey up. They raced from the room, Kelsey in retreat and Russell in victory.

'That was marvellous! I knew you had it in you!' Russell cried, clapping Kelsey on the back. 'Didn't I tell you to just be yourself?'

Butley Priory by Amber Atkinson

This location provided inspiration for 'The Ghost Room' during a drive to Rendlesham Forest. By following the B1084 to Capel St Andrew Road, you will come to the beautiful Priory and estate. New to the area, I took a drive to explore the forest and drove past the Butley Priory. The architecture and landscape, combined with some historical research gave room for this story to grow. I enjoyed celebrating the idea of the haunted parts of a beautiful area of Suffolk.

The Ghost Room

The flowers nearby don't bloom anymore and the neighbours in Butley seem to hold secrets of the history of this place a little too tight.

I rolled over onto my right side while my eyes adjusted to the early spring sunrise. Looking at the clock, I saw it was already 6.30am. I got dressed and lifted my cleaning caddy off the scratched oak floors. Delilah gave a loud squeal followed by a growl and buried her head under her paws. I was glad to see her sleeping calmly. Recently, Delilah had started pacing at the foot of my bed all night in response to the doors and windows that slammed open and closed. No matter how many times I checked they were closed before I went to bed, the noises in the night had become worse since Mr Bower's great-great-granddaughter had returned to Butley for her wedding.

Leaving Delilah sleeping, I made my way to the east wing of the mansion. Having finished the west wing yesterday, it was time to clean the Honeymoon Suite. The room I had been putting off the most.

There is an ancient story that belongs to the suite. Five hundred years ago, a woman called Lilibet Bowers died suddenly in this room and her fiancé, the Butley Prior at the time, never recovered. He was found hanging there just three days after her death.

I pulled out the rags and furniture polish and got to work cleaning. Opening a top drawer of a bureau, I pulled away the yellowed silk handkerchiefs it contained and saw a small wooden box. Carved into its lid were the letters, *LB*. I opened it to find a silver ring with three yellow diamonds. Thinking nothing of it, I placed the ring onto my left ring finger. I snapped the box shut and placed the box inside my front pocket of my Carharrts. I finished cleaning and felt a breeze coming from the other side of the room. I turned to the windows, but they were all shut.

It took me hours to clean that day and it was late afternoon by the time I came downstairs where I grabbed my coffee inside a travel mug.

'Delilah, come on girl!' I called for my two-year-old Harlequin Great Dane.

Since I agreed to take a three-month residential in the Butley Gatehouse, Delilah had been my only reprieve from the oddities that came at nightfall. Graduating from university class of 2055, I had higher hopes for myself than trying to reopen a gatehouse as a wedding venue.

The village had been mostly abandoned a couple of years ago, due to what the local papers announced as *unexplained paranormal activity.* A letter had arrived for me and had brought to my attention things I hadn't been able to explain. Inside the envelope was a piece of notebook paper, folded over several times, creased and aged. The edges were yellowing, and it smelled of Amber Leaf.

To the landlord of the premises: You have something belonging to Mr. Bowers, 1555. Once returned, Butley will be at peace.

Delilah led the way out of the heavy front door and onto the property, off lead as usual. She did a few joyful bounces in between the muddy puddles.

'Not too far!' I called to her as if I thought she would understand me.

Looking ahead I took in the views. With the fog still hanging low, Delilah and I took our usual morning route from the Priory to Low Corner and back. A round trip of thirty minutes which was just enough for Delilah. With her close to me, and nearly all the way home, I veered us towards the Priory where the door had remained bolted shut since the coffin of Mr Bowers had been placed there.

I had struggled to find out much about why it was closed until the pub landlord down the road, recently returned to the village to try and make a living, said the Priory was taken as Mr Bower's resting place. Delilah gave a low bark and I jumped.

'It's just a stick, leave it.' I said firmly. We carried on our usual route and Delilah picked up her pace heading for the Priory. I ran after her, unsure of what had spooked her. After five minutes of jogging ahead through the deep woodlands surrounding the village, we reached the boarded-up Priory. A beautiful old building made of a mixture of flint and stone, it stood in an area of unkempt landscape and tall, dying trees.

Delilah jumped onto her hind legs and pressed her nose against a tiny stained-glass window in its flint walls. She gave a sharp bark.

'What's the matter? Down girl.'

Inside the building, I had been told, was a smaller room, a living quarter where supposedly Mr Bowers had nursed his broken heart after his fiancée died. Mr Bower's coffin had been placed there not long after being dug up from his initial grave, as those who committed suicide weren't allowed to be buried on consecrated ground.

The rotting trees surrounding the building left much to be desired. I was never one for ghost stories, but here inside this building was what Graham our grounds manager had called The Ghost Room, due to hikers mysteriously getting lost or going missing after trying to enter.

Delilah and I began the long walk back to the groundskeeper's cottage where I had been staying while trying to renovate the main house for the first wedding to be held there in a decade. Above, the sky was quickly filling with dark clouds and the winds seemed to pick up out of nowhere. I realised we needed to head back.

I felt my phone buzz and quickly answered it.

'Hello?'

'Come back at once,' a hoarse whisper answered back at me. I felt I could almost feel the voice's breath.

'Who is this? Come back where?' I answered.

Suddenly a large rotting tree trunk fell over just a few feet in front of me, separating me from Delilah who whined loudly. I tripped over one of its smaller branches.

'Delilah!'

The dog stepped back and jumped over the tree meeting my side.

The sky had grown even darker, and I realised nightfall had come very early. I felt down the side of my trousers, found my travel torch and turned it on. I had lost my phone when I fell and it was nowhere to be found.

I gave up on finding my phone, gathered myself and turned back towards the Priory, thinking we might shelter from the oncoming rain. I grabbed Delilah's collar and kept her close. I looked down at my hands covered in mud, apart from the ring on my finger which now looked to be glowing.

I stopped to catch my breath by the widest tree I could manage to find in the dark, closest to the Priory, Delilah nearly knocking me over. My ankle gave way beneath me, and I heard the loud snap of a branch beneath my soaked leather boot. I covered my mouth as if that motion would make my entire body invisible, unsure why I felt the need to be hiding from sight.

I watched as the tree branches violently threw themselves at the unopened door of the Priory. I looked behind me once more before standing. Now the rain had started, and I began to shiver in its onslaught.

'Let's go, girl!' I cried out to Delilah, and I got ready to run.

I ran as fast as I could to the wooden door of the Priory which flew itself open as soon as my feet met its threshold. Thick plumes of dust surrounded me, and I began to cough.

I heard a loud slam.

I flipped around on my heels. The door was shut, and the locks turned on their own.

'Is there anybody here?' I called out with a crack in my voice, grabbing Delilah's collar, drawing her close to me.

I shone my flashlight and found the second locked door rumoured to be The Ghost Room. I walked over to it and with a loud creak, just like the other door, it opened itself.

I could feel my heart pounding out of my chest and exhausted, I sat down on a metal-framed bed inside the room, covered with a sheet. Delilah slunk under the bed. There were large pieces of old furniture, covered in thick layers of dust. As I drew my light across the various black-and-white photos propped up on mirrored frames, I saw a man in the reflection of the frames.

'What have you brought me?' he said in a low whisper.

I still couldn't make out where the man was in the room. I felt a sudden pain in my hand and realised the ring felt tighter. I tried to take it off, but it wouldn't budge.

'Why did you do this to me?' the man continued.

Before I could answer him, the wind began howling so loudly, I couldn't hear myself think.

'Stop it!' I screamed and crouched beneath the legs of a table.

'Give it to me,' the voice commanded.

'But I don't have what you want!' I answered back.

A sinister laugh was traded for the fierce winds that froze my cheeks.

I shone my flashlight and realised what I thought was a table was a base for the coffin of Mr Bowers.

I stood up and stepped slowly towards the coffin. The ground beneath my boots began to shake and the cracks in the floor widened. As fast as I could, I turned back on myself and calling Delilah to come, I ran for the heavy door, hoping it would open.

'Leave us alone!' I screamed. My legs felt heavy and I could no longer feel solid earth under me. With no explanation, my body was thrown back towards the bed, and I fell onto its mattress where I lay unable to move, or scream.

The first thing I felt as I woke up was the warm soft licks of Delilah's tongue on my face. I opened my eyes, sat up and gasped.

'What on earth?'

Delilah jumped off the bed and scratched at the door. My bedroom door? *Thank heavens*, I thought, feeling the warm honeyed light of day pouring in through the leaded light windows.

I heard a light knock on the door.

'Ma'am, the electrician is here for the survey.'

'Thanks, Graham,' I called to the ground's manager.

I rubbed my eyes, shook my head to clear the memories of my dreaming.

'Come on, girl,' I said to Delilah as I dressed. 'I think it's high time for our morning walk.'

Delilah let out a strange cough. I turned to her and saw her cough again, as if she was trying to rid her throat of an obstruction. She coughed again and I heard a clinking sound on the floor. Covered in Delilah's drool was a silver ring, with three diamonds, bouncing the sunlight onto the walls of the master bedroom.

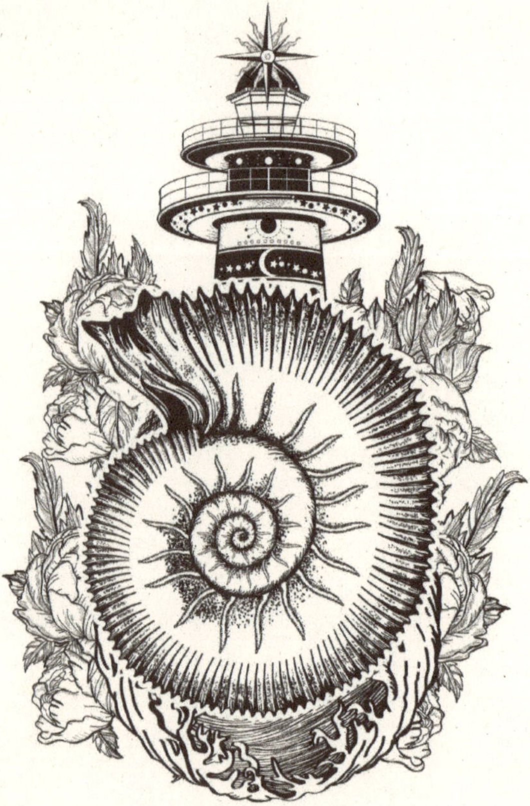

Orford Ness by Caroline Roberts

Orford is a small village on the Suffolk coast to the east of Woodbridge. The ness itself is a sixteen-mile piece of land that lies between the River Alde and the North Sea and can only be reached by boat. In its long and mysterious history, the ness has been home to a top-secret military testing site, the buildings of which still remain, and to various lighthouses; a feature that is now gone forever. Taking inspiration from M. R. James, whose ghost stories have become synonymous with and perhaps even a part of the Suffolk landscape, I wanted to explore the tension that exists between man and the force of the sea, an important theme in James's work. This is nowhere more symbolic than in the form of the lighthouse, especially at Orford Ness. I have tried to emulate James's direct, matter-of-fact narratives whilst retaining my own, more lyrical writing style, and to follow his movements through the story to an ending of inevitable horror.

Taken by the Sea

The ness at Orford is a strange place. A desolate spit of land at the Suffolk coast standing between the sea and the mainland. Nature thrives there, having lately reasserted itself amidst the derelict remnants of a secretive past.

This story is my mother's, told to me a year ago, although how long ago is of no consequence to you, I'm sure, except perhaps to establish the time that has passed since the telling of it.

It had been a bleak day and the eddying grey clouds had recalled it to her. That and the damp, salt-scented air that hung beyond the open window of her bedroom. My mother wished for me to know the truth about her husband's death a year or so before, though much of what I relay to you now was by necessity her husband's account of events.

He was not my father, but a man whose easy, charming smile had belied an arrogant and opportunistic nature, though she said she had resigned to tolerate this for the company he provided her in later years. They had not long lived in Orford, retiring somewhat late, having wrenched themselves from the distractions of Ipswich.

The whole village, it seemed, was in a state of mourning for *the old lady*: an affectionate term used for the lighthouse that stood on the ness for well over a hundred years before finally being dismantled to save it from the same fate as its predecessor. The old, old lighthouse had been taken by the sea, its wooden timbers clawed and splintered by the clamouring waves, the flotsam hauled ashore by pilfering seamen.

These scavenged timbers had provided precious materials for cottages in Orford, such as my mother's. The prize catch of an entire door, the lighthouse entrance, had been dragged from the sea and fitted into a gap in the narrow hallway that opened onto a steep wooden staircase leading to the cellar. Or so my mother's estate agent had claimed.

Suffice to say, fresh air and idle days had made my mother's husband restless. Local pursuits had first been met with derision, but he had found some kindred spirits in a village pub and taken to evenings of darts and dubious conversation.

One heavy drinker began to rave of the cod catches that abounded on the other side of the ness, the dogfish and rays that appeared in the spring and the fishermen who could provide them. He hinted at the private buyers, assured by his company of male friends, who would pay over the odds.

For many weeks at dusk, my mother's husband would steal away towards the shore. On his return, she would hear the knock and bundle against the cellar door as he stashed illicit fish catches in great barrels, ready to sell them on. Enthused by his fortuitous hobby, he worked hard to increase demand. The more he asked for, the more the fishermen took from the sea.

On several occasions, my mother warned him to be more respectful, but he had shown little care, turning away or lifting his paper to express indifference.

One day, he began to complain of a leak in the hallway pipes. He described a dampness on the cellar door and fine pools of water collecting in the corners. She checked again and again, but there was no wetness anywhere, only a faint briny stench that she attributed to the fish.

In the gloaming of an April evening, my mother's husband went out as usual to meet his supplier. As he left the encounter, with his catch tucked under his jersey, the early evening dusk was stolen by darkening clouds that hung over the spit. He squinted through the gloom and halted. A tall, shadowy form appeared where the lighthouse had once stood, flashing as though the light was turning its head towards him.

He rubbed his eyes, shaking the notion out of his thoughts and raising his hand to look again at what must surely be a trick of the moonlight. But the faint outline appeared once more in the wide flash of a ghostly beam.

Daring to look away, he hastened on, slipping on the boggy grass by the huts and hurrying past the boats towards the road.

Back at the cottage, he collapsed in his chair and relayed the events of the evening to my mother.

'A warning, surely,' she told him. But he gathered himself, poured a large rum and blamed a bad barrel at the pub.

At bedtime, she called out to him uneasily.

'Shall I put out the light?'

'Attending to business!' he grunted from the hallway. 'I'll be up soon enough.'

But he never came up that night. In the grey shiver of dawn, the bed was still neat and empty beside her when she awoke.

Downstairs in the hall, her bare feet were met by a chilled pool of water. Her hands grappled with the softness of damp, salty timber as she pushed open the cellar door.

And there she found him.

Great knots of glistening seaweed were wrapped around his neck, its swollen pods bulging at the throat. His head was bent back in an unnatural repose and his mouth was held in gaping fury by a glut of sand. Stones and tiny ancient fossils protruded anxiously where his teeth had been. His wild, staring eyes betrayed a startled horror.

It was as if the great sea had washed through the room and spat him back out.

The fish were gone.

Mother is gone now, too, and the cottage seems empty without her. I confess that I never believed her story – her husband's death certificate suggested natural causes and nothing unusual was declared in the coroner's report – but I am glad to relay it to you now. I have never noticed any dampness about the cellar door, but on bleak days, when eddying grey clouds gather over the spit, I watch the fishermen taking out their boats and wait for a glimpse of the lighthouse.

Rendlesham Forest by Mike Laurence

Rendlesham Forest lies four miles from Woodbridge and was planted just over one-hundred years ago. Just to the west lies Sutton Hoo, the burial place of an Anglo-Saxon king, and to the east, a ruined Augustinian priory from the twelfth century. During the Second World War a central section of forest was cut down and turned into an RAF airfield, and during the Cold War, the US Airforce took it over.

In December 1980, several witnesses saw strange lights in the forest. They also described unidentified sounds and even reported a silver craft with tripod legs. The USAF took these reports seriously and an inconclusive investigation followed. It was noted that Orford Ness lighthouse, five miles away, or the planet Mars rising in the east, could have explained some sightings and the sounds could have been wild animals. But for many, these dismissive explanations failed to convince.

The 'Rendlesham Forest Incident' has remained a potent source of mystery and speculation ever since. Carl Jung, the famous analytical psychologist, regarded the Flying Saucer phenomenon as 'visionary rumours' feeding into quasi-religious myth-making suited to the technological era; angels replaced by alien machines. Geography is strongly associated with myth-making. Visions become associated with places of pilgrimage, be it Lourdes, Varanasi, or Glastonbury Tor.

The forest now has a well-signed UFO trail, and as evening falls, anything feels possible.

Rendlesham Forest, 1993

The Ford Fiesta had seen better days, its yellow beams barely illuminating the bumpy forest track ahead. Sean snorted and rolled down the window handle, spat out into the dark.

'Couldn't you afford a better motor? Thought you'd have a Beamer or something.'

'Think that'd be your style, Mister Dealer.'

Toby was having a bit of trouble seeing straight. The track kept splitting then converging, hard to tell if it was geography or neurology.

They slowed to a halt and spilled out of the doors, laughing. The car stereo pumped out sub-bass into the darkness. They sat under a tree, its hefty trunk rising far above them, and listened to a bunch of tracks. The idling engine coughed, cut out, and the headlights dimmed further before fading away. They sat and chatted more in the dark, in companionable silence, as the woodland sounds took over.

A bark in the distance.

'Jeez, what was that?'

'Just a deer. Thought you lived round here?'

'Yeah, but not in the friggin' woods. I need another spliff.'

Toby lit up a ready-rolled from behind his ear and inhaled deeply.

Sean lay on the ground looking up at the stars.

'They're coming,' he laughed and stared up at the tree trunk behind him. His throat shone pale in the moonlit wood. 'I can hear them.'

Toby focused his ears on the night noises, a distant roar at the edge of hearing.

'I think it's just the London line.'

The sound faded.

'It's the Big Note, stupid.'

'Big fart more like.'

Their laughter echoed back from the forest around them.

Time passed.

The woodland sounds grew louder, a crack of twig, a screech.

The moonlight faded behind high cloud. A cool dampness rose from the woodland floor through Toby's denim. Their mood settled, the night closed in.

A flicker though the trees caught Toby's eye. He looked straight at where he thought it was, but then it was gone. He looked away, and it was there again, in the corner of his vision. 'You OK?' Sean enquired.

'Didn't know you cared. Did you see that?'

'Probl'y some perv in the woods.'

'No, it was too high up.'

They both turned in the direction Toby indicated.

'Reckon it's a plane from the airbase.'

The dark, the wood, no longer felt so comforting.

Toby shivered.

'Anyway, it's gone now.'

Sean continued to look intently at the sky.

'Remember when we camped out in your dad's back garden in London?'

'Yeah, we didn't sleep a wink, then bunked off school next day.' Sean's voice was smiling, and his hazy moon face turned to his friend and for a moment, in the low light,

Toby thought he saw another set of features speaking his friend's words.

They chatted some more; the parties, old schoolfriends, the geeks and the tossers, the girls they fancied.

'And I thought you were a complete wanker. Your trousers didn't even reach your shoes.' Sean snorted.

The banter eased and quietness slowly replaced their jaunty memories.

Toby gradually became aware that he could see some of the trees around them more clearly.

Hesitantly at first, then with a growing certainty, a point of light slowly rose between the trees, shining in their direction. Toby heard Sean's breathing quicken.

'I don't like this. What was in that grass?' Sean's voice was over-deliberate.

A feeling of pressure, he later recalled, like when a plane descends, affected Toby's ears, and his hearing seemed to diminish. The place they were in felt like the centre of something weird and deeply disconcerting; as if a huge change was about to happen, or a door was opening on a great and dizzying height.

As if in a dream he tried to answer Sean, but his speech was reflected back into his vocal cords, recirculated like a familiar childish nightmare, crying after his mother as she walked away; yet no sound emerged.

Then a second light, yellower, rose to meet its companion and started to drift slowly in a wide circle around them, as if observing, thinking.

'Jeez, I'm not waiting around for this, whatever it is.' Sean's voice sounded shockingly clear.

Toby watched as his friend stood unsteadily and began to run away from the lights, along the soft track, footsteps dulled by dead pine needles.

With a hiss, the yellower light took off in the same

direction as his fleeing friend, moving between trunks, dodging and dipping.

'Sean, wait, don't be daft.' Toby rose on legs numb from sitting on the cold ground.

His legs seemed to resist him as he stumbled along the track, the yellow light disappearing in the distance. He stopped to catch his breath. The light behind was now brighter and a terrible buzzing filled his ears.

The next he knew, his cheek was pressed to the cold forest floor. Time had passed, and his head ached. The wood, the darkness, the faint sounds around him were all that was left. He got up and searched for his friend.

Hours later, dawn came. Sean was gone.

For years after his friend's disappearance, Toby would screw up his courage and go to the forest, on the same night of the year if he could. There were rumours from friends that Sean had gone abroad, but even Sean's dad had no clue of his whereabouts. He'd even been reported missing to the police. But Toby knew different.

Sometimes he'd come across twigs arranged in a pattern, or maybe an area of pine needles disturbed.

One such night, he saw the flickering again, at the edge of his sight. He sat under a tree, hard to tell if this was the exact spot, but it felt right. His head rested back onto the trunk, and the headache grew, the usual screwdriver in the eye.

He must have nodded off.

There was a figure in the dark, standing a few yards away. He couldn't make out the features, but the stance was familiar.

'Sean?'

The figure dissolved into branches and backlight.

Framlingham Castle by Milena Ristic

You might wonder how a girl from Serbia, born and bred, can have any connection to Suffolk, and better yet, to Framlingham Castle. To be fair, I don't particularly understand it myself, but I did feel a strong pull towards this castle. I believe it has to do with my hometown, whose claim to fame is that once it was the capital of our medieval kingdom. The town is home to Smederevo fortress, the main attraction of the town and a stunningly beautiful stronghold where I spent many weekends walking around with my dad. It is no wonder then, that I was attracted to Framlingham Castle as a location for this project, with its fascinating history, open court and picturesque mere, all calling to me to create a personal, meaningful story. This castle held something within its walls that reminded me of home, no matter how far away.

I went to Framlingham Castle fairly recently, one Saturday with a new friend I had made just three days earlier. We took the B1077 route straight from Ipswich to Framlingham. We had a lovely breakfast in a café in town, visited the castle and walked to the church as well, all on a rainy, windy day. Not even the weather could have spoilt the trip.

Come Closer

You seemed so far away that night, more so than on any night before. Too far away from me. It was that weighty and hollow feeling, an absence in my stomach, a gaping hole in the centre of my chest, the feeling I have been carrying around for a decade now. Why did I think it would remain that way? Why didn't I believe?

We got there at eleven, the steely darkness was our friend, the rain a nice touch for the atmosphere. It was Jay who suggested Framlingham Castle for our next investigation. He didn't know of my connection to the place, he didn't know that the castle was our favourite weekend spot. A place you took me to so we wouldn't talk, we could just walk around and be silent. I loved coming here because I felt like a little princess, I felt like those walls were mine, like all the stones were a part of my own house. And I just adored walking all along the wall walk imagining myself living there, walking alongside Queen Mary. I don't know what you felt then.

As soon as Harry the night guard opened the heavy doors to us that night, I felt a warm gust of wind surround me, like arms wrapping my body in a hug. And then, there was the strong smell of cigarettes mixed in with the rain, a punchy and familiar scent, straight from my dreams, from my memory.

'Do you smell that?' I whispered to Jay.

He didn't even register. He was picking up the camera and our equipment bag. *The ghost gear*, as we called it, and directing Harry on where to put the GoPros.

'I'm gonna need one on the wall walk, one on the ground floor. Did you say the attic has activity? Maybe one there. Another one upstairs. Be careful with that one. When did you say the figure of the woman walks around?'

'Oh, not just any woman, Margaret Brotherton. She was actually quite remarkable, I told you to look her up, right? She was a countess in her own right and I've seen her. Leanne and Ruby saw her, too. She walks around the inner court. Once, I even saw her up on the second floor right in front of the exhibition room. I was all alone on a shift and out of the corner of my eye, I could just make out ...'

'Harry, I'm sorry, could you please save that for the interview? We might have to do a voiceover, too; the wind is really picking up now. Let's set up. Rose, you all good with that bag? Put up your hood, your hair's getting wet.'

He started walking towards the museum entrance inside the court just on the left, Harry following behind, all jittery and exited. I didn't know why he was so enthusiastic. I didn't have the heart to break it to Harry that after the episode aired on YouTube, he might as well start looking for a new job. There was no way Heritage would allow him to keep working here. Especially after doing the one thing that was forbidden. Letting a ghost hunting crew in through the front door was the equivalent of inviting a vampire into your home. But at the same time, I knew that he wouldn't miss the opportunity to be a ghost hunter himself. That's why he was so easy to convince, back in the pub. Jay barely finished telling him the plan.

So, there we were, the three of us, in the empty castle. Jay and Harry set up the cameras, the motion sensors, the EVPs.

I always feel things. I do, it's why Jay came up with the show idea, it's what we bonded over. I always feel other people, other spirits. I'm not afraid. I hear their shy voices, their shadowy footsteps. I listen to their whispers and groans. Their moans and cries. I feel their tears. I sense their dead cold. I sense with all my senses. I let them use me, I let them show themselves through me. They always come through. But not that night.

I was not afraid, but they didn't come. They didn't, but you did.

'Rose, come on. Where do you want to start? Upstairs? The wall walk, maybe? We can film you in front of that "BEWARE" sign, that'd be a great shot.'

'I can't Jay.'

'What do you mean you can't? Come on, do your thing, baby.'

'I don't feel anything here.' I was feeling too much.

'Impossible. Maybe you just need a bit more time. I believe in you. Look, why don't I film Harry and you go get some air, huh?'

'Yeah, I think I'll do that.'

I left the castle in haste. The fresh air, yeah right. I could only smell ash and smoke, like the scent that was left after your house burns down. Along with you. The round walls of the castle felt suffocating, too tightly wound around me, a heavy curtain. This castle was too ringlike, a stony crown. I exited the inner walls and took a right, down the wonky stairs, heading for the meadow. I was wearing my old boots, the ones you bought me a time long ago. I stopped growing then.

I was paying attention to my feet, careful not to slip on the muddy and uneven ground, thinking of ghosts and how they always stay close to their places, always in that one spot. They can follow to a certain border and never cross. No matter how much you want them to. I was caught up in my own treacherous mind, so I wasn't aware that there was someone else there. It was only when I reached the open meadow and looked up toward the old college that I saw them.

They stood there looking across to the mere, a girl and a man, their backs turned, a small hand in a big warm one, a wonky ponytail flying on the wind. Her head turning to look up at him, struggling to catch his gaze. What is this man thinking? Was he angry at her? Well, were you? I let go of your hand just the once, to signal, to make a statement only a ten-year-old can. I let go and you didn't look back. You felt it but didn't look back.

'Come closer,' a shadow puffed into my ear, like it was exhaling smoke. 'Come closer to me.'

And I did, Dad. I started approaching your familiar figure standing all alone on the meadow, your leather jacket glimmering in the moonlight. I came closer and you turned. You were young, as young as I knew you. You were there, and well.

'You loved me, and I loved you, I did, I should have said.'

'Turn around and I will follow. I will always follow you,' said the spirit.

You seemed so far away that night. I came closer and you did, too. Now, you are always so close, right here.

Blythburgh by Jeni Neill

The B1125 Blythburgh crossroad is reached easterly from Walberswick, westerly from the A12, with Blythburgh to its north and Theberton to its south. It is curiously unmarked, bearing neither wooden signpost nor mention of the burial site that it is. The wind cuts over it and there is little around it but field and hedge.

Its anonymity suits the vagueness of its history. For here, in September 1750, Tobias Gill was hung in chains to slowly die having been found guilty of Ann Blakemore's murder. She was found dead with no cause of death or sign of injury ever discovered. Whether they were known to each other is unrecorded. Apparently, the verdict was influenced by local accusation and that he was found drunk close to where her body was found.

Tobias Gill was a black man serving as a drummer in the 4th Dragoons, based in this area, most likely very unpopularly, to combat smuggling. The parallel of the black service men building the airfields in this same region in the Second World War struck me as I devised my tale. Whilst I hope they were better regarded, history often informs us otherwise.

Ann Blakemore's ghost is said to run by the crossroads around the anniversary of her death, whilst some report a headless Tobias driving a coach pulled by four headless horses. In truth, his body was left swinging from the gallows for years and eventually became the ground where it fell. Whether they were lovers or strangers, they are now connected in history and have inspired me to draw them together for my tale.

The Yellow Ribbon

Dusk steals the daylight. Alice's hopeful wait at Blythburgh crossroads rapidly dulls, too. If only she could wish Manu back. Why did he insist on meeting her parents today anyway? She hopes his uniform isn't damaged from her stepfather's attack.

If he's going to come back, he'll come to the crossroads.

Alice considers biking to Leiston base. He could be there by now. But what if her stepfather realises she's gone out? Vulnerability pokes like a stone in the overgrown grass she sits in. Drizzle brings the clouds to earth. The only other presence is the darkening silhouette of foliage and storm-split trees.

A sudden ghostlike swoop, low across one of the lanes, spooks her.

'Bloody owls,' she mutters, drawing her cardy tighter around her.

Her mounting apprehension steals the familiarity of this, their regular meeting spot on the outskirts of the village. The age-old tales of Tobias Gill flash to mind. She imagines his decaying body, hanging in chains on this very crossroad island two centuries before. Blythburgh folks' babbling tongues the only suggestion of his crime but once hung, even their accusations had faltered.

No mark was found on Anne Blakemore's body. Tobias could have been innocent of her murder.

He was black, like her Manu. She recalls her stepfather's racist words. Tobias' ghost comes knocking again but Alice swipes it away with her tears.

She jabs at the soil with her house key, loosening, agitating. She won't be scared off. Not by man or ghost. Her key hits something hard, lodged within the earth's layers.

Metal?

She feels for a stick to help further the hole, her fingers straining to reach. Soil gets under her nails. The object seems stuck, but she's fixated now, pulling it free of its earth bed. It looks like two rings, tied together with some sort of string. *Am I supposed to find this?*

Pocketing her find, she glances at the time. Reluctantly she returns home. Gingerly she turns her key.

Please God, don't let him hear me coming in.

Shoes off, she creeps up the stairs, passing the argument beneath her in the lounge. Her stepfather's words make her linger at the top.

'Oh, shut up, woman. She'll end up like Anne Blakemore. She's playing with fire, stirring things up. Folk don't like it.'

'That's a threat you'd better take back, John. You need to change your thinking – and so do *folk*. You won't create that same sorry story with my girl and her Manu. What will you do if he won't go away? The way you're talking, I wonder what lengths you'd go to?'

'Don't rile me woman. Know your place. He's not wanted here. And I'll teach him it, Liz.'

'You're talking about a lad, for God's sake. A lad come over here to help us win this war. A lad who loves *my* daughter. Yeh, and his skin happens to be browner than yours, John.'

The waver in her mum's voice catches Alice by surprise.

She runs down the landing, her tread covered by her stepfather's thunderous cry,

'His skin ain't my skin at *all*.'

Alone in the bathroom, she wishes she could retract her stepfather's words. They aren't words she wants any part of. She wants to sack them up, drown them in the Blyth.

Picking angrily at the dirt in her nails, she leans over the basin to wash the treasure she found. If only it had been a genie's lamp, she'd wish herself to Manu. Her nausea is like the grime swirling in the sink, but fascination takes over as her gentle rub removes layers of time.

As the dirt slips away, two initials are revealed. *T* on the larger ring and an *A* on the other. It's a slim, weathered ribbon that links them, not string. It disintegrates, leaving only faint yellow threads in the basin.

Could this T be for Tobias? And maybe A, Anne Blakemore? Was she really his sweetheart?

The rings warm in her loving hold.

A ripple of light shimmers in the mirror, but the curtains are drawn.

Swaying a little, Alice creeps to her bedroom, wanting to sleep.

She wakes, disorientated, surprised she dozed off. What woke her? There's a smell, faint but building in potency. It's tender, sweet. Like roses.

Something stirs in the corner. *A breeze? From my closed window?* It is unusually cold. She looks to the rings on her bedside. Fresh yellow ribbon binds them. Thoughtfully tied with a dangling bow. Her heartbeat rises to her throat. Then she realises what woke her. The shouting has moved upstairs.

'See Liz, I *told* you she'd sneaked out. There's muck all over the sink! I'll show her bloody muck …'

Leave. The thought stamps with authority as if it's been ordered from beyond. *Grab your stuff and leave. Be with Manu.*

Her stepfather enters her room, throwing on the light. Her mother's right behind him.

'Don't hurt her, John. Please don't …' She's frantic, desperate.

Think fast. Think clear.

John spies the rings by Alice's bed. 'What the …' Storming over, he snatches them up, then recoils. The flesh of his clenched fist is melting. Howling in pain, he manages to fling the rings to the floor. Alice sees them roll. The yellow ribbon remains in place. John's palm is branded with the burn of a link.

'Are you a bloody witch as well as a whore?' he bellows.

Alice's mother pulls her close.

'You both want to get it, do you?' he screams, belt in hand, pounding round the bed. A putrid exhale stops him. Alice smells it filling the air, like unseen breath, and yet somehow she knows it's come to protect her. Grey dust, like the shadow of the sink's soil, begins to form a shape. Its willowy movements hold them all spellbound as it shifts from a cloud of hovering particles to become woman, or is it man?

The shape compresses, intensifying to a dark knot that erupts through the window, taking John with it. He crashes to the earth below.

Alice races to the window to see her stepfather dragging his crumpled limbs, suffering any agony to escape the menace that's upon him. Whimpering, he disappears into the night.

The rings call to her. Loosening the yellow ribbon, trancelike, she slips the smallest on her finger.

No, it can't be.

The larger ring's initial has changed to an *M.*

Is this meant for Manu?

Blythburgh by Lou Mary Carr

Take the road towards Wenhaston opposite the Queen's Head at Blyford. Stop just past the church, before you cross Blyford Bridge. Then take the path beside the River Blyth, heading east.

Breathe. The mudflats, marshes, and reedbeds of this evocative landscape are lonely and beautiful. Drift in silence beside the water with only the whispers of the rushes in your ears. 'The Wonder' came from a fascination with the process of writing historical fiction. How people from the distant past are both real and unreal. The spaces these characters leave for imaginings, and how untold, urgent stories are voiced through the contemporary writer. I wanted to write about being haunted by my characters.

Ethelthryth is based on a real woman, the daughter of King Anna of the Angles. Anna ruled over a prosperous and largely peaceful East Anglia in the mid-seventh century, and his daughter was married twice, before becoming an abbess.

'Here Anna was killed,' the Anglo-Saxon Chronicles bluntly states, referring to the location of my story. But it's all conjecture; no body was found, no record kept. More is known of Ethelthryth. She went on to found a community in the Fens that would later become Ely Cathedral. It's a couple of miles walk by the river to Blythburgh, with its glorious church and more than its fair share of legends and spirits. But don't be like my narrator and attempt this walk as night begins to fall. Who knows which Anglo-Saxon spirit you may disturb!

The Wonder

'We don't call it historical fiction anymore,' Anton says.

He offers a little smirk as he stirs his coffee.

Anton has a Suffolk weekend place, close to Blyford, where he has met me in the Queen's Head. Anton is vague on what we *do* call it, now we don't call it historical fiction.

I'm still bristling from his unpunctuated message in the middle of the night: *in your part of the world* – sheep emoji – *coffee & chat?* He has also, during this 'chat,' got the name of my second novel wrong and repeatedly referred to my work as dark ages feminism, which is, apparently, something we are moving away from.

He studies his screen, grinning to himself.

'She's a wonder,' he says, chuckling. 'Our newest author,' he explains, although I haven't asked. 'Her first novel came in a *vision*. Right in front of her eyes, would you believe?'

'I would not,' I say.

He frowns, snaps his laptop shut and drains his oat milk latte with a grimace.

'A wonder,' he repeats, offering me a thin, lacklustre hand. He's got his leather satchel over his shoulder, cloth cap on artful hair, and is halfway to the door when I realise what he's done.

'Offer still stands,' he calls, one foot in the pub car park, 'if you fancy a bit of mentoring. Lend her your decades of experience. Now you've time on your hands.'

And just like that my literary agent, Anton, has dropped me.

Naturally, my car shudders at the mere suggestion of starting. I rest my forehead on the steering wheel for so long it leaves a dent. It's growing dark. I live nowhere near Blyford. I do not wish to be spotted by Anton, walking his possibly groomed and bijou dog, as I wait for rescue in my wreck of a car, bought with my advance all those decades ago.

I get out of the car, wrap a scarf around my neck, pull on my coat, and drift across the road to the river.

'Mentoring,' I ponder, climbing the stile by the languid water.

I take the path between the river and marshes as the light leaches from the sky, rolling up into skeins of purple and iris and deep, dire blue. Perhaps even a young 'wonder' can discover something new? The ground is soft beneath my trainers, my ankles brazen in the evening chill.

'Hello,' I say, standing aside for a man to pass. He stares through me to the church and the road in the distance, but his springy spaniel comes up for a sniff.

'Hope,' he calls, reprovingly.

I assume that's the name of the dog.

I watch them drift away, green-dun shades of jacket and fur misting into the marsh grass and the reeds. To my side, through the bare, spiked alder branches, the merest notion of a shadow stretching over the brown water.

I walk on, into the glint of gold lights in the distance. It's not far to Blythburgh, which is where I decide to head towards. I remember walking this path – probably before Anton was even born – to research my first novel. 'Ethelthryth' it was called. An Anglo-Saxon princess and her father. It did not come to me in a vision.

Perhaps I can get a room in the pub there, sink a bottle of wine, pull the covers over my head, and forget I ever called myself a writer.

I stop because I think I hear a cry.

It's just a whisper of wind around my ears, hesitant at first, building until it becomes insistent and chill. And then, beside me, that surmised shadow. But now the shadow has a body, and the body is not my own.

Decades pass. Centuries. Millenia. Women wore different clothes then. Drapey robes and cloths embroidered with gold and vermillion and madder rose.

The woman doesn't turn around, doesn't look at me.

She pulls her hood over a glean of russet-brown hair. She is standing deep in the river, the periwinkle blue of her dresses blooming around her waist. The woman's shoulders shake beneath her cloak. She's crying.

I look to where she looks, to the horizon where the river widens into a great swoop of water, where the sky shatters and is in an instant, black. A thudding terror surges up through my chest with the briny scent of water, forcing the sound from my ears until it bursts onto the soft, sighing sibilance of the rushes. And another sound. The faint crackle of fire.

I know it before I see it.

A longboat aflame; a carved wooden craft whipped by tongues of orange and white and a brilliant cinnabar red.

A funeral farewell floating on the horizon.

'Ethelthryth?' I ask.

She turns, studies me in silence. She wipes her eyes and her garnet-red rings shine against her pale cheek.

'How do you know me?'

'I wrote you,' I say, not knowing if she will believe me – if I believe myself. 'I told your story.'

She nods and arms aloft, wades through the river, her

bracelets and pendants chiming like tiny bells. 'And in your telling, where is my father?'

She shivers, wraps thin arms around herself. 'Did you have him killed? Did you let my father's body burn on that boat, like a heathen?'

I shake my head.

'No?' Ethelthryth smiles, eyes bright.

'I saved him.'

I'm about to tell her what I wrote, but she puts her finger to her lips. She reaches out a hand and I take it, warm palm on warm palm. Behind her, the flames from the boat subside, doused by the falling night. Stars remain, sharp as sword-tips.

'I'm sorry no one reads it anymore,' I say.

'It's enough that you imagined it,' she replies. 'Thank you.'

Suddenly, I'm beside her, the rush of the river bitingly brilliant around my toes, my thighs. Together we take longer and longer strides, breathless and laughing, splashing up droplets into our faces.

'You're not real,' I whisper.

'Possibly. But then again, what is? That's the true wonder of it all,' she says.

Dunwich by Matthew Wiles

Dunwich sits between Leision and Halesworth along the east coast of England, within the Suffolk Coast and Heaths AONB (Area of Outstanding Natural Beauty) and along the North Sea coast. It is a nineteen-minute drive from Saxmundham to the village via the A12. The beach of Dunwich can be found along the edge of the coast, only a short walk from the village centre via St James's Street.

Dunwich was originally a thriving coastal city and trading port before and during the thirteenth century but was swept away into the sea during a great storm in 1287. Now, the city sits at the bottom of the sea, England's own Atlantis. There have been stories of ghosts haunting the surrounding area, of bells tolling in the distance from a church resting under the sea as the ground gave way to the tides of time. It is these stories, and this lost city, that has inspired the tale presented to you, of ghosts and questions and echoes of the past.

The Vanishing

Beneath the waves of Dunwich, there is a town dating back to Anglo-Saxon times. The lost capital of the Eastern Angles. Legends say it was victim to a storm of storms, ravaged by the winds and torn to shreds by the heavens themselves ...

Of course, as we all know now, Dunwich wasn't just lost to a storm; it was swallowed whole by the sea over time, becoming Britain's own Atlantis. In the time between its sinking and its rediscovery, there has been a veritable army of ghost stories that have sprung up, a legion in fact. Ghostly figures lingering on the beaches, shadows moving freely in the moonlight, and other tall tales to spin and weave for those gullible enough to listen to them. Nowadays though, most people are happy to write off these stories as merely misunderstandings and superstitions from a time when such things ruled the world.

I am one of those people. I do not believe the stories. I find them to be nonsensical. And yet, I cannot deny a strange fascination with them. A curiosity. I am intrigued how a lack of understanding of the world around oneself – especially back in the days when faith was used to explain the seemingly unexplainable – could result in so many fables and myths.

And it's where I find myself now, on a journey across the Suffolk landscape, seeking to find those tales and explore them, to dissect and deconstruct them. I want to find the truth within them, to peel back fiction to reveal reality.

It is here that I will begin my book, a tome on old tales and how they came to be, and, just maybe, I will find some answers to my own questions that I have always had about, well, everything.

Dunwich is where I will start.

I have discovered there is little information to gain from the few people who live here in the remaining village. The lights in the houses are off. Are they all out, or are they inside, hiding from me? If so, then why? The few people that do open their doors merely provide information that I already know. Frustrating. I've been all around the local area, even over to Southwold and Halesworth, but I've got nothing for my book. Less than nothing, in fact. Nothing close to ever satisfying my need to know what is on the other side.

No. No. Stop it. Control yourself. Control … yourself.

I let out a sigh and sit down on a bench overlooking the beach. Purple heather flowers intermingle with long whisps of green and yellow grass. The beach is long, sandy, and stony at the same time, always being wetted by the incoming waves. The endless sea glistens with light from the setting sun. The pink-kissed sky is mixed with oranges, blues and blacks rolling over the earth like a curtain. The distant sun reminds me of a canvas painting, cresting down over the horizon.

Then someone sits down on the bench right next to me and begins to speak.

They say their name is ... actually, I don't ... I don't remember what their name is. I can't, it feels like I can't. Hell, I don't think I can even recall what they look like. But they did speak to me.

It is the first time that anyone has spoken to me in a while.

'Why are you here?' they ask.

'To research Dunwich,' I answer, before quickly adding on, 'The missing town of Dunwich, I mean.' Why am I suddenly speaking to him? Maybe I'm simply desperate for any scrap of information. They are, too.

'Why?'

'To look into the ghost stories around it.'

'And why is that?'

I glance at them. Their features are fuzzy in my memory.

'Just curious ... I have my reasons.'

'Really?'

'Yeah.'

'What are they?'

'Does it matter?'

'Everything matters.'

I looked down at my hands. I'm silent for a long time.

'When I was younger,' I began. I'm not sure why I began to speak. It just all started to come out on its own. 'I was in an accident. I don't remember the specific details of what happened and even if I did, I wouldn't want to go over them now. But I was close to death. To dying. To simply slipping away from life, and I swear, I saw something on the other side.'

The stranger nods as I begin to recount what came before.

'I know I did; I did see something. I don't know what it was, the memory faded as soon as it formed for some reason, but I know that I did see ... *something*. I just don't know what. It's been plaguing me ever since. I've been trying to cure that, to figure out what I saw. Every textbook, every record, every sighting of ghosts and angels and legends of old gods and beings from beyond human comprehension; all in a quest to know what awaits us when our end comes.'

I keep talking, unravelling the thread.

'I've never believed these tales ... but I want to. I want to believe there is something beyond death, and the ghost stories of Dunwich would've shown me. But now ... now ...'

I feel the stranger's eyes upon me. I've only just realised how much I've shared with them for reasons that I cannot understand.

'Why am I telling you this?'

'You tell me.'

'Who are you?'

There's a pause.

'Who I am isn't important. It's who you are that matters, that, and what you're going to do with yourself.'

'What does that mean?'

'Come on, you can't just spend the rest of your life chasing shadows. If you spend the rest of your life worrying about what will happen after death, you'll never learn to enjoy life. Trust me, you only learn to appreciate something when it's gone.'

'How do you –'

'So, tell me. Is this really what you want? Do you want to spend the rest of your life chasing after shadows? Or do you want to enjoy the life that you have now?'

I stay silent for a long time.

'Who are –'

I turn my head, but they are gone.

I look up to the pink and orange horizon and watch the rolling waves of the sea sparkle in the setting sun. Underneath that sea is a town, swallowed by the waves and filled with potential for answers.

Then I look down to my lap, at the opened book and the blank pages inside.

I close the book.

Maybe some stories are best left untold.

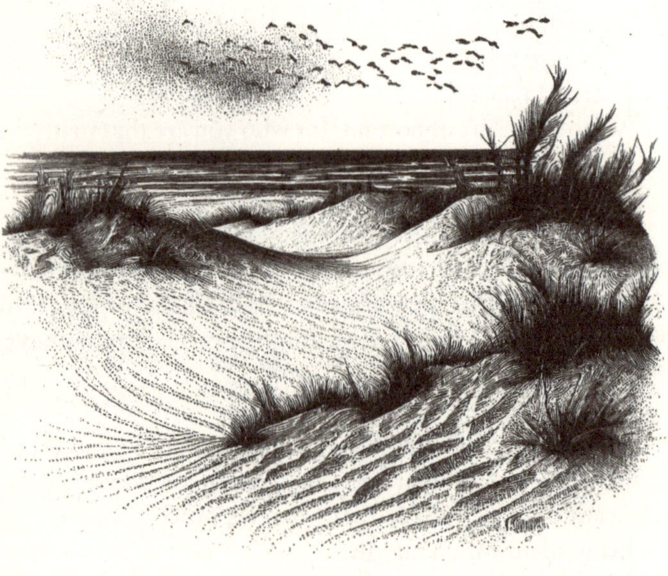

Covehithe by Rob Sadler

Take the A12 north to Wrentham and turn right to join the B1127, then take the first left to Covehithe and follow the Roman road for about two miles. Soon, the gothic arches of Saint Andrew's Church rise from the flat fields of Suffolk's edge with an eerie sense of foreboding.

In researching this story, I was intrigued to learn of provost-marshal William 'Smasher' Dowsing and his anti-iconoclastic antics during the English Civil War, hence the desecration of superstitious imagery and art. Many of the graves are undecipherable now, due to centuries of salt-lashed gales, but one austere-looking crucifix always draws my attention, due to its lack of inscription. Who were these people of nameless headstones and what of their ancestry? The religious fervour during the English Civil War led me to examine how the humble cross, in the form of a necklace, can act as a talisman from past to present. The question I am always asked, concerning the washed-up seafarer, is whether he is of this life or not. Well, that is for you to decide.

Soon, the church, its graves and perhaps the hamlet itself will be lost to the sea, so I endeavoured to bring to life the tangible feeling of déjà vu that I always sense when visiting this haunting corner of my home county. The old haunts of Suffolk are steeped in historical figures and ghostly tales, their lost souls and sunken crucifixes forever ebbing on the tides of Covehithe.

Tides of Covehithe

1643. Lying face down in the ebbing tide, curds of sea salt lap my bleeding ankles. The storm has claimed the ship which was to take me away from this country of heretics. My allegiance and faith bear me great ill, through the eyes of Oliver Cromwell.

Thin sunshine heralds a milky dawn. I see two armoured guards appear at the top of a cragged cliff. Upon noticing my drowned form, they begin their hasty descent. Frilled pantaloons and head armour suggest that they are of the protectorate cause, but they do not strike me as *The Ironsides* who bring so much fear to the Royalist troops. Grabbing the scruff of my sodden sack tunic, they drag my lifeless body to the base of the crude wooden steps that lead to the clifftop. Hauling my limp carcass feet first, I count the thumps of my head against each splintered step before the men fall to their knees in exhaustion at the top.

The sound of their drawn swords serrates the gentle whoosh of the ebbing waves below as they cut the crucifix from my neck. My body is propped against a stone cross at the graveyard's edge of St Andrew's Church. Above me, the pale linen sky hides the gulls that circle us. This is my parish, my birthplace, my death. Behind the headstone, a stack of ancient bricks almost fills a large arched window, where once an easterly dawn bathed its congregation in Godly rays through brightly stained glass. The guards kick my lifeless body.

'How shall we dispose of the corpse?' one asks.

'Burn it.'

'The provost-marshal is already at Wrentham. There is not time.'

'Throw the body into the crypt.'

'Guards!' There comes a cry from the lane. 'Man your posts! William Dowsing is here to free this parish of all its superstitious images. You will assist him forthwith.'

I am dragged inside the church, the blood from my wounds easing my body's passage across the ebonised inscriptions of the dead. The guards reveal their true intentions to my dormant ears.

'He, Dowsing, by virtue of a pretended Commission, goes about like bedlam breaking glass windows, mistaking the liberal arts for Saints, defaces and digs up the floors of our chapels, not regarding the dust of our founders who likely were buried there. We must resist.'

The door to the crypt is raised and my body is flung into an icy tomb.

The ferocity of glass shards smashing upon the floor above arrests me from my fading breaths. A line of arrow-slit windows, carved in the shape of the cross, bathe the crypt with just enough light to reveal a silhouetted figure of a nun stooped over me. She is wetting my cracked lips and bathing my numerous body wounds with a stinging ointment. I try to speak, but a skeletal hand reaches out and purses my lips together with a touch as cold as death itself. She places her thumb and forefinger on my weary eyelids, closing them.

A cold gust peppers my face with coarse sand, woodsmoke fills my nostrils with a rejuvenating spirit. My limp body is once more propped against the same headstone of the now bloodied cross.

The crypt door lies burnt out before me, clouded by

smouldering embers, pulsating orange in the warm breeze, its iron ringed handle aglow with the heat from the Protestant vandal.

The heads of the guards who imprisoned me are kicked down the crypt steps by the nun who tended to my wounds. My suspicion of their ill-fitting attire and battle-hardy credentials suggest that these were Royalist infiltrators, disguised as puritan guards to save the church of its catholic artistry and smash the head of William Dowsing instead. Their severed torsos are stacked in a savage crisscross pile next to me, so I prise open their rigor-morticed palms to search for my talisman, my cross, to no avail.

The nun and my crucifix are gone forever now. I am alone with the dead.

Present Day. I have been dispatched by the Home Office Ministry of Justice to meet with the last warden of the parish at the coastal hamlet of Covehithe, where Saint Andrew's church is teetering dangerously close to the edge of the crumbling cliff face. My mission is to document the gravestones and assess any possible exhumation of the bodies for re-burial before they are claimed by the sea.

My grandmother always maintained that we hailed from this part of England and there is a strange familiarity to these endless flat fields, impending skies, and gale-lashed cliffs.

Approaching the ruins, the churchyard gate swings upon its rusted hinges with an eerie foreboding. The swirling drizzle wraps a cold easterly fist around the hollow arches of this crumbling edifice, like flames licking at a funeral pyre. Crouching down to view a headstone cross at the graveyard's edge, I run my smooth palm across its lichen blistered inscription, but I am unable to feel any name or date. Referring to my documents concerning the grave, I am aware of a shadowy figure in a hood at the cliff edge watching me from afar.

Raising a tentative hand in feeble acknowledgement, I accidently drop my pen onto the grave. Stooping to retrieve it, my hand grazes the sharp gravestone edge. I jolt as the hooded figure appears beside me and places a small, chained crucifix into my bloodied palm, closing my hand with a slow morbidity. I look up into the hollow vacuum of a faceless void, who then forces my dripping fingers to the centre of the stone cross. The now relentless rain mixes with my blood to slowly reveal an inscription.

My own name. My own death.

Dazed and confused, I find myself stumbling along the shore below.

Two guards appear on the clifftop above.

Who was it who died here?

My ancestors are the grains of sand beneath my feet. I fall face down in the ebbing tide, the crucifix painfully embedded in my punctured palm.

A hooded figure points out towards the cruelling sea.

Lowestoft by Sheena McCallum

Lowestoft is the most easterly point in the United Kingdom; tucked out of sight in the north-eastern corner of Suffolk. It once thrived thanks to its fishing industry and its status as a Victorian seaside resort, complete with piers, promenades, and golden sand. In more recent times, North Sea oil and gas and, latterly, the renewable energy industry have been important for the town.

Lowestoft was heavily bombed in both World Wars and the decline of the fishing, oil and gas industries led to unemployment and a decline in the town. Whilst other Suffolk resorts such as Southwold and Aldeburgh have remained popular, Lowestoft's star has faded. Efforts are afoot to encourage investment and regeneration projects seek to recover something of Lowestoft's former glory.

I had my own reasons for avoiding Lowestoft, that were both nothing to do with and yet inextricably linked to its more vulnerable side. This story explores my own personal ghosts against the backdrop of a coastal town.

I would urge you not to avoid Lowestoft for as long as I did or dismiss it as yet another seaside ghost town. It has glorious sandy beaches and long promenades, the wonderful (and free) First Light Festival around the time of the summer solstice and a history and heart well worth discovering.

It can be reached via direct train from Ipswich or

Norwich or found at the very end of the A12 if travelling by car. Just head due east.

First Light

Lowestoft had become a spectral town in my mind. I hadn't been brave enough to visit for three decades, too haunted by memories of my father to think rationally about why I wouldn't go there. Then, last winter I reluctantly accepted an invitation to the town's First Light Festival, a midsummer celebration of East Coast light held on the South Beach. I knew, however, that I would need to conquer my demons first, and alone.

I approached the town centre through the February drizzle and from the South Beach side. I walked slowly, counting forty-six consecutive lonely benches, without a single sea-gazing occupant, between Claremont Pier and the East Point Pavilion. One bench offered a long-dead bouquet in cellophane, a tangle of yellow Sellotape holding it in place. It occurred to me that, in thirty years, I had never left flowers in my father's memory. I didn't even know where on the river outside town he had died. Or where his grave was.

I saw two large red crosses on the gantry structure across the road ahead of me; meant for cars, not me, but still I hesitated before walking on. I crossed the harbour bridge, making way for two women on mobility scooters, heavier rain now running down my face.

My father had lived alone in Lowestoft in the late 1980s and I had only ever known the town through his eyes and my reluctant and infrequent visits. My teenage self would wander aimlessly with him around streets darkened by the storm clouds of his depression.

I now wanted to look afresh and, remembering advice to always look up to get to know a town, I stopped to do so. Above the Papa Johns' billboards and an empty shop called Angel were two floors of rooms in a Victorian building; weeds grew along the balustrade, a satellite dish, wonky blinds, and flimsy drawn curtains suggested occupants, and I could just see a shadowy bed. Dad's bedsit had been similarly rundown, but I didn't think it had been in this part of town. On the opposite side of the junction stood a once beautiful Edwardian building with intricate plaster-work. The bottom floor held a large, abandoned café-bar and on the two floors above, some windows were glassless and boarded up whilst others displayed grubby net curtains. Perhaps Lowestoft was still the town I remembered.

I crossed the junction to Station Square and wondered about all those souls who had arrived and departed from this town. Lowestoft is not somewhere you visit by chance, it's literally the edge, a liminal space between the land and sea. I watched the pensioners nursing cups of tea in Wetherspoons before I turned down London Road, the town's main shopping street, a street I was certain would act as a conduit to the past.

A small altercation broke out in a group of homeless people sheltering in a large derelict shop doorway. Tempers calmed as quickly as they flared, and loud cackles rang out from one of the women. Did Dad ever hang out with groups like that to pass the day? Would that have been preferable to a cold, barely furnished bedsit for someone who had in happier times loved the company of others so much? I shivered.

Derelict stores were interspersed with charity shops and banks. A young couple with a toddler in a flimsy pushchair sheltered in the bank doorway as the man scraped furiously at a scratch card. I looked again, recognising the Lloyds Branch where I had tactlessly flaunted my first ever cashpoint card to withdraw five pounds so that we could buy some rolls and biscuits to take back to his cold bedsit. He was incredulous that his daughter should have a cashpoint card; he never had.

I walked a little faster, and turned down a side street, wondering how long the lone, female, taxi driver at the rank, leafing through a wordsearch, would wait for a fare.

I noted the National Spiritualist Church in a small, shabby hall on my left. Would they claim to be able to connect me with his spirit? I didn't believe they could. And it was irrelevant in any case; the board said *closed*.

I passed the bus station, unsure which direction to head in. An impulsive left turn brought me to the drab concrete buildings and car parks of Clapham Road. Primary-coloured panels on the façade of the library shone out, in contrast to the large oppressive Job Centre in a municipal office block opposite. He used to complain to us that its staff and 'the system' were not kind to him as he struggled with benefits and being too unwell to keep a job.

Cold and wet, I welcomed the idea of warming in the library. Unlike the streets outside, the library was alive, although nobody was reading or holding a book. Tables on both floors were mostly occupied. Teens played chess, a large group of adults with learning difficulties played boardgames, two older ladies, one struggling to speak, hunched over a computer, and two women discussed getting people onto various programmes, agreeing a need for *exit strategies*. Did he seek shelter in here, too? I tried hard to place him here at a table, writing one of the many letters he sent us. Any letters I still had were buried deep in a box in storage. I made a mental note to look for them.

I sat in the library for an hour, loathe to leave, trying to anchor my father here. The courage I had found for ghost-hunting in cold, empty streets was fading fast. I left, retracing my steps back to the seafront and the neutrality of the East Point Pavilion. The Pavilion is testimony to regeneration, a beautiful and arty space; but cold and empty in February. An invitation for the outside world to visit on a sunny day, rather than a sanctuary for locals.

Sitting with a cup of mint tea, I stared at dark grey sea wondering what I was searching for, and why? There were so many other places where I could retrieve memories of happy times spent with my dad. It wasn't Lowestoft's fault his life fell apart here, and I didn't want to remain fearful of the distant past. I realised that he wouldn't want me trawling the streets for sad memories.

And when the summer eventually came, I reclaimed Lowestoft once again. This time with my own teenage daughter. We went to First Light Festival. We watched the sun rise, and we danced to music barefoot in the golden sand. Dad would have loved it.

Student New Angle Prize 2024

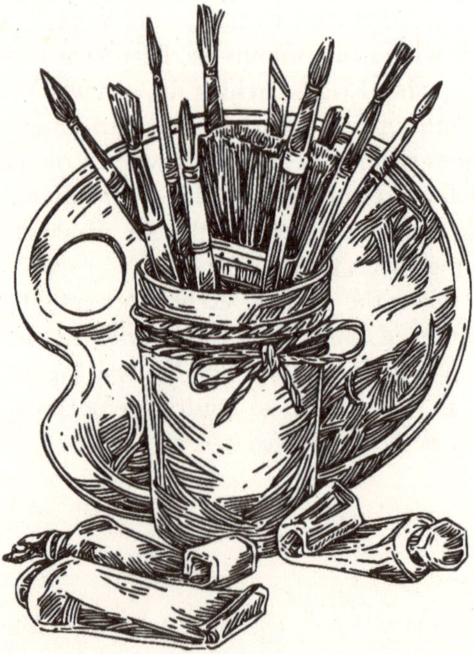

Colours of Our Days by Jeni Neill (Winner of the SNAP Prize 2024)

Although the Capital of the Fens, Wisbech, like most of its surrounding fen, suffers from social-economic neglect. I gained no energy from this once rich marsh that was my childhood home. Its vast sense of space, being a wide, monotonous edge, isolates it and its people further still. Returning to East Anglia with my husband's work, we moved as close to the Suffolk border as possible, knowing its picturesque shores and more visual history. Suffolk is on the periphery of the Fen, with slopes and softer lines. But still I wondered if I could bear it. Why was I destined to be here, only a short distance from that original fen heart, firmly connected despite denying my attachment? An awareness came to me on a particularly bleak rail replacement bus journey, whilst staring despairingly at endless flat. I needed to make peace with this land, I couldn't escape it as it was part of me.

Researching the fen history, I embraced what it once was, appreciating what has influenced and formed it and, most especially, its disregarded people. I think that's when, almost self-consciously, 'Colours of Our Days' must have seeded. Painter Jack realises there is power within his connection to the land: rather than being tied to our landscape, we are crafted by its lines and take its shape. We can be its voice. We may feel suffocated and marginalised by it, but these are words to work with and to explore. When we need to speak out, trust in our voice and speak out, using our landscape as our brush or pen, being truly as one.

Colour of Our Days

I am John Gedge from Yarmouth way, known as Painter Jack. My grandpa caught the herrings; nan fret till he got back. They made kids who waltzed the dancehalls, ran the seafront clubs. Turning from a life at sea to sit and draw the land, my fingers curled around a brush, not the rope of Grandpa's hand.

My eyes sharpen to the shift of light and its ever-changing hue. They look to paint and frame a tale; one known by just a few. I watch still and patient in sun and wind and rain, gathering thoughts on what I see – what's gone and what do remain: walk with ghosts through rows and denes to see the past again.

Marsh harriers now share space with red kites' turns and calls; wellies flop up highstreets, sheep painted for festivals. We shift, rebrand, dilute, take less, hoping to make more – like fish and plant's diversity, where fen edge meets saltmarsh shore.

I am John Gedge, with paint brush at the ready. But my viewpoint's squint is limited unlike those gliding birds of prey who sense harsh wind approach before the forecast's shared, hear the tinkle in a spider's web, feel dew before it reaches grassy blade. My perspective needs to alter, work with all this change – for Painter Jack can grow and his subjects rearrange. Our scenes may shift, escape my sketch, charcoal, brush, and pen, but safely etched in memory I know fen light will shine again.

I've tried to lay honest marks, share what I can see, but sometimes from one day to next, coastline is lost to me. Ronald Blythe unwittingly kept note of all we've lost, but now it goes too fast to catch – ways of life crash like waves too roughly tossed. History keeps drowned Dunwich, hidden Sutton Hoo, but I don't look to stories, I'm drawn to shades of blue; linear lines of sky, land, sea, touched by the same tinge. Neither Constable's comfort nor Gainsborough's green capture the spirit of this marginality.

All creation, whether learnt, adapted, real or old, needs time to settle in. My eyes share what's been and gone and will return once more. Nothing is new, shot with no root. Seed comes from what has been before. So, fret no more when change and loss have us take our heads in hands, with the warnings so contrary to our rulers' greedy plans. Our footprints on the sand shift too fast to be observed: but recall toddlers' stumble until determined they emerge.

So here I be, Painter Jack, woke to a new dawn. I'm down Yarmouth Pier today, paints ready for a storm. Pa and Ma pull mobility scooters up to see the colours of their days: these colours true as the weather, told in my blues, blacks, mauves and greys.

Wenhaston's Doom by Lou Mary Carr (Runner-up of SNAP 2024)

I discovered the Doom painting in Wenhaston's gorgeous little church while researching my story for the *Suffolk Haunts* anthology. Wenhaston's Doom is a stunning example of a medieval wall-painting depicting the Last Judgement, which would have been a common sight in churches of the time. This visceral, visual narrative of the end of the world gave the congregation something to ponder when listening to the sermon. Wenhaston's Doom was originally positioned within the chancel arch, above the painted rood screen, in front of the eyes of the sinners who could not ignore the judgement on good and evil it portrayed.

Wenhaston's Doom is dated to around the early 1500s. It was whitewashed at the time of the Reformation and left standing, disguised, on the rood beam for the next few centuries. In 1892, Wenhaston church was refurbished, the whitewashed planks of the hidden Doom removed and thrown into the churchyard to await disposal. But it rained during the night, washing away the covering, and revealing the Doom in all its glorious detail. Go take a look at it now, in its new position opposite you as you enter the church.

In pondering the Doom, I wanted to write about guilt, shame, but also the power of creating your own future within the confines of a restricted life. I don't know who painted

Wenhaston's Doom. But I'd like to believe there is a story – hopefully with a happy ending – surrounding its creation.

Wenhaston's Doom

The soul must weigh more than the souls of two imps. That is the judgement, the Doom. It is painted on timber above the candlebeam, above the rood screen, nailed within the chancel arch at the front of the church for everyone to fear. It is clear; one pure soul, two imps. Whichever weighs less is damned. There's the devil behind the scales, scroll in his left claw; *now for what is lacking may you give pardon for your sin.*

Margery's soul has always lacked weight. That is the judgement.

The creation of Wenhaston's Doom began in 1515, when Margery was a child. It was fiddle-faddled through her girlhood, stood fallow for want of funds as she married, was made real to Margery only when they hired a new journeyman to complete it. The final strokes were to the fangs of the leviathan that looms above Margery's head. He painted them last night. 'The first were for Christ's rainbow, though that were a mistake,' he said. 'Surely you should leave the best for last?'

The journeyman's name was Cornelis. He came from the Low Countries to look on the Doom with fresh eyes. Bring it *closer* to perfection. 'For only God can judge perfection,' the parson warned, 'as only He can judge your sin, Margery, *depart from me, ye cursed, into everlasting fire …*'

But Margery kept returning, to watch Cornelis with his

long, thin fingers touch the tip of his brush again and again to the woodgrain. To smile as ultramarine dots wavered, held their flawless form in the curve of the Virgin's eyes. Margery listened to Cornelis speak of his home by the river. He held her as she talked to him.

Margery's soul is not smooth and silky like the soul resting weightiest in the pan. She is more like the imps, Cornelis had said. He didn't mean harm, but she turned away, thinking of the vermillion hew of Hell and the gaping jaws of the fish; *a flame goeth out of his mouth*. Why paint an inferno if it does not exist?

'But you are the kindest, fairest woman,' he said, and 'does this feel wrong?'

Attentive, it felt. Considered. Rich.

'Come home with me,' Cornelis said, eyes the azurite blue of the heaven-seat and the sky. The clear answer was no. But there had been time to weigh the question.

'Just look at the Doom,' he told her as he said goodbye. 'I have altered it.'

Between Michael and John is the devil, the same dark temptation, but Cornelis has repainted the devil's arm in its ragged sleeve. It now rests above the scales, ready to nudge them down in his favour.

See how easily the balance can be tipped? That is the judgement; a delicate art. Margery laughs in the silence. She casts one last glance on the Doom and runs from the church, towards the boats, with a joy as light as an imp flying free from her soul.

Rooted by Sheena McCallum

I wanted to write about Suffolk and belonging. I live in a remote and beautiful part of north Suffolk, but it isn't always the easiest place to belong or put down roots. I am interested in how we might strive to be absorbed by a landscape.

A few miles north of the village I live in is the beautiful Waveney Valley, typified by gently sloping meadows and rustling poplars. Immediately around my home is a patchwork of large arable fields and big Suffolk skies. There are no main roads to the village, just a network of lanes linking to other ancient and remote villages. Common land is a local feature and nearby commons come alive with orchids in spring and grazing ponies over the summer.

The area is not immediately accessible (you need to dive in from the A140, A143 or A1120) but it is worth the effort for walks, bike rides, historic churches and, of course, traditional pubs. The villages stretch from Hoxne (site of the largest find of late Roman gold anywhere in the Roman Empire), to Wingfield and Syleham (home to Dodie Smith's inspiration for Cassandra's castle and the church where Ed Sheeran was married), Fressingfield (for the wonderful Fox and Goose restaurant) and down to Laxfield, with the timeless Low House, a traditional, thatched pub (officially named The King's Head) which serves beer and drinks from a tap room at the back. There is no nicer place on a summer's evening!

Rooted

I try so hard to root myself in the ancient north Suffolk countryside that I have brought my family to. I survey the fields of sugar beet and winter wheat, the ancient commons, and tiny ill-kept lanes, where tufts of grass grow in place of cats-eyes. I want to reach deep down into its dependable soil and anchor us.

I attempt to understand the landscape by walking footpaths through fields of barley that stretch to Mendlesham in the long distance, its mast stood sentinel to the south. I run, sharing tarmac with roadkill, and struggling for breath as oil seed rape tingles in my nostrils. My heavy footsteps startle resting hares into action. I drive and watch morning mist clearing above cow-grazed meadows.

However hard I persist; the roots fail to take hold. I've seen no sign of myself in new buds or spring growth. Curmudgeonly villagers sap my energy; evangelical parishioners don't welcome woke outsider folk. Non-native species don't flourish here.

I want Suffolk to be the place I belong; I spent much of my childhood here. But I cannot forge a lasting connection with this hidden, land-locked countryside where everything, bar the sky, is solid, slow moving, and heavy footed.

Perhaps I should look eastwards, towards Suffolk's estuaries. Snape and Iken on the Alde, Pin Mill on the Orwell, the

Blyth estuary, and magnificent Deben; they make my heart soar. Their constant flux and fluidity fuel my dreams and I feel energised by the light. Boating communities conjure hopes of adventure and migrating birds promise foreign lands.

I wonder whether you can simply attach yourself to somewhere or whether you need to be able to stake a claim. Only a quarter of my ancestors, my blood and bones, hail from Suffolk; the opposite side of Suffolk to where I am trying to establish roots. Maybe I should look south to their graves in East Bergholt, in the Stour Valley's Dedham Vale with its pastoral meadows and gentle beauty carried along on quiet river currents.

Where else might I belong? I dismiss my Essex ancestors and look further afield to the Scottish and Cumbrian landscapes and coastlines of my father's line. The wilder side. Lives of great drama, highs, and lows, led at full speed and played out against heart pumping and endorphin generating landscapes. I fear that as much as I love dramatic scenery, I can only ever be a visitor there; I don't have what it takes to flourish. The westerlies are too extreme, and I would be blown adrift.

I shall persevere with Suffolk, but I wonder if I really want to put down roots. Or whether I am duty bound to give my children roots. I like being free and untethered. I think they do, too. The ability to float at will is underrated.

The Habitat by EJ Daniels

Midway through my time at high school, Ipswich Academy decided to move to a new building. My memories from visiting the build's archaeological dig are hazy, and that's exactly why I wanted to write about it. There was a strangeness about being in this big open field interrupted by the effects of machinery that I've never quite experienced since, and that I never want to forget. Also, the fact that we were building a lizard habitat felt strange. I never saw any lizards, and even if I had, how were they to know where they should move?

Prompted by the book's title of *Suffolk Haunts*, I combined this childhood conspiracy theory with my present-day love of poetry and eldritch terror to create 'The Habitat'.

The Habitat

Back when my old school decided to move,
they did an archaeological dig
to make sure that they didn't harm precious
antiquities in the process. Long dead
grass was torn up in strips by their immense
machines, leaving a labyrinth of mud.

They brought a few of us kids to their mud
piles, us and our headteacher, so the move
could involve all of us – well, the immense
number of students meant they had to dig
around a bit. Most wouldn't be seen dead
at that site. Reputations are precious.

So, there we were, four of us, the precious
students, the 'smartest.' My image was mud
at that point. Worse than mud. If I had died,
I'm sure no-one would have noticed. They moved
the four of us between the holes they'd dug,
towards a clearing. 'Build something immense.'

We asked what they meant – they said the immense
structure was to house the lizards – precious
lives that would be rehomed thanks to the dig.
'They can't simply burrow into the mud
when the school has been built. They need to move
to a new habitat, or they'll be dead.'

We built. They left. A sound made us stop dead.
A rumble. Not from them. Something immense.
Something terrible. Something old. We moved
back, watching, hearts racing, as our precious
habitat made of sticks and logs and mud
barely held. God, why did they have to dig?

We knew it. We all knew it. They had dug
something up. Something buried, assumed dead
long ago. Something that had lain in mud
for an immense length of time, so immense
that we'd forgotten. But now, its precious
ground had been disturbed. It wanted to move.

Beneath mud and concrete lies something immense,
but Ipswich Academy still stands.
We students at the dig were never precious,
It's why they chose us to build the damn
dead wood barricade.
It refuses to move.

You can still see it through the fence.

Shingle Street by Harriet Sellers

As the title suggests, the poem is set at Shingle Street. When I first moved to the area, Shingle Street was a place that really captured my imagination and made me feel like I wanted to make Suffolk my home. It was also the place that reignited my passion for creative writing. The poem is slightly ironic in that I hadn't had much interest in birds when I first visited Shingle Street, hence the reference to 'twitchers' rather than ornithologists, but have subsequently developed a genuine appreciation for them, especially the mysterious short-eared owl, which is the bird described in the final stanza.

Shingle Street

The car stops. We pull on our hats and gloves,
and strike out across the gloomy saltmarsh.
A motley group of twitchers block the path,
armed like soldiers with their Gore-Tex and glass.
We hurry past, an embarrassment of nods and smiles
curious to know their purpose, but too polite to ask.

A serpentine lagoon runs parallel to us on the left,
cut off from the sea by a protective embankment.
We skirt around the edge of the brackish waters,
scanning the surface for a seal or green-winged teal,
but with little success: few creatures have the mettle
to withstand this storm-wrought wilderness.

The ground undulates gently beneath our feet,
dimpled by rising tufts of saltwort and sea beat.
Herring gulls flap overhead like clean washing.
Eventually, we reach the top of the sea wall and
look down the slope at the greedy little waves,
as they toss the variegated pebbles like popcorn.

We scramble inelegantly down the steep bank
and linger a while on the rocky carpet below,
mesmerised by the rhythmic motion of the tide.
To the left and to the right, the shifting contours
of ancient stones gleam in the pallid sunlight:
flint, quart, quartzite, ironstone, chert, and grit.

The muffled sound of a distant bell buoy chimes:
our minds turn to thoughts of tea and hot toast.
Cold and tired, we head back along the ridge,
past the marram grass, glowing violet-bronze
under the reddening sky, past the birdwatchers,
clinging like barnacles to the same lonely spot.

As we near the road, a pale shadow swoops down,
gliding with the ease of a newly sharpened knife.
Its bullet-shaped body a blur of white, buff, and brown,
its yellow eyes blazing like giant sunflower heads.

The twitchers aim their lenses as we load up the car:
they have been waiting for this moment all day.

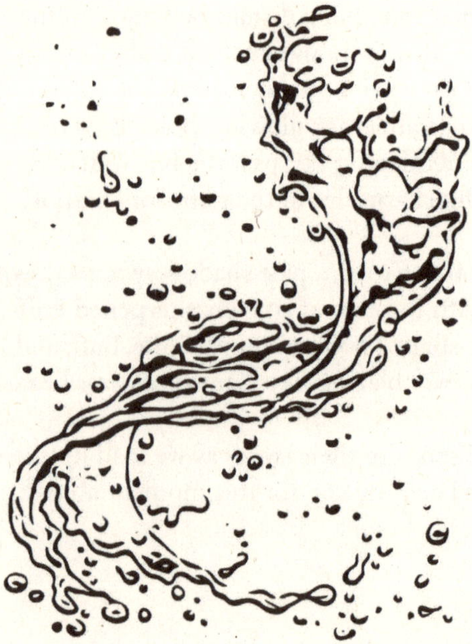

You Can't Hold Back the Sea by Tracy Davies

I am a mature student, and in an effort to improve my writing skills for my BA Counselling degree and my reflective writing, I decided to go back to my childhood comfort place of Shingle Street. It is a little-known stretch of the coast. Not famous like Orford, Aldeburgh, or Southwold, but that adds to its charm and wilderness. While I was there, I paused to reflect on how sadly the landscape has changed so dramatically, and that my daughter will never know it as I did. The result was the piece I wrote in my journal. I then decided to enter the SNAP competition just for fun, never dreaming that I could ever be considered as a finalist. Much amusement and support from my peers, also I hope I have inspired others not on English courses to also have a go and seize every opportunity that the University of Suffolk has to offer.

You Can't Hold Back the Sea

Reclining on the beach at Shingle Street, on our Suffolk Coast, my mind drifts, lulled by the siren song of the waves lapping the shore. Thoughts float to the surface as I reflect on the Green Week Campaign. I am warm in many layers, yet my face stings from a biting wind. I am watching gulls circle aimlessly above me, when my thoughts circle in my mind, considering that you can't hold back the sea.

Memories surface of a long-ago school visit to Dunwich. It felt as if we were travelling so very far on a distant adventure, now just a relatively short car journey. Yet, I am still haunted by a model in the village museum which showed where a whole community used to be, all vanished, swallowed up by the storms. A local ghost story of a church tower with the bell clanging under the sea, which legend says can be heard ringing a haunting warning on stormy nights.

Bawdsey coastline, where there were once beaches I used to play on as a child, are all now eroded. Only a jawline of ugly concrete teeth attempts to stop the waves eating the shoreline.

Houses cling to the very edges of cliffs, fighting valiantly to remain. Why were they built so close to the edge? Once they were in the heart of a village, where have the families gone?

Woodbridge, my hometown. Previously a boatyard, with

smells, noises and craftsmen working. Now a manicured waterfront shopping parade. Metal barriers are the developer's protection, but the river is an ancient power seeping through. The hills opposite, where the Anglo-Saxon Kings rest on high ground, must wryly look down on our modern arrogance, greed, and folly.

Have we still learned not to fight nature? End pollution and encroaching housing estates on land that floods. Build nuclear power stations on heathland and coastline with roads like arteries blocking and choking the way through the unending hubris of man.

We can learn from the past, it's not too late to sympathise, and respect nature. What changes an older generation must have witnessed. Our only hope is that the next generation can repair the damage, find creative solutions for the flood plains and broads, to protect and respect the wide range of habitats for wildlife and preserve our wonderful county of Suffolk.

Yet despite all this – nothing and no one can hold back the sea.

Writer Biographies

Polly Crosby writes gothic historical mysteries and her debut young adult novel came out earlier this year. Her latest historical mystery, *The House of Fever*, is out now.

In 2018, Polly won Curtis Brown Creative's Yesterday Scholarship, which enabled her to finish her debut novel, *The Illustrated Child*. Later the same year, she was awarded runner-up in the Bridport Prize's Peggy Chapman Andrews Award for a First Novel. Polly received the Annabel Abbs Creative Writing Scholarship at the University of East Anglia. Polly can be found on X and Instagram as @ WriterPolly. Her website is www.pollycrosby.com

Gabrielle Stones is a writer and poet living in Suffolk. She has had poems and short pieces published and has found a new passion for writing short stories for young people. Gabrielle is currently studying on the MA Creative and Critical Writing at the University of Suffolk, continuing on from her BA. She is currently working on a series of realistic short stories to relate to young people in today's society. In her spare time, she works for a young people's charity as well as finding time to focus on her passion for reading and writing.

EJ Daniels is a nonbinary writer with a love of all things dark. They are in their final year of the BA (Hons) English and Creative Writing at the University of Suffolk, for which they are writing a collection of short horror stories inspired by the Grimms' fairy tales. A portion of their work has been performed at INK Festival 2024. At present, they are in the process of writing a young adult novel about vampires, a monster that has fascinated them since they were young.

Ellen Freeman is an author and poet from Suffolk. In 2023 she completed a Writer's Residency at the Van Gogh Museum and is currently working on a collection of essays and poetry inspired by the artist's life. Ellen was shortlisted for the Canterbury Festival Fiction Prize in 2022 and longlisted for the Student New Angle Prize in 2023. Ellen is currently studying on the MA Creative and Critical Writing at the University of Suffolk and graduated from the Open University's BA English Literature and Creative Writing programme in 2021. Ellen is the author of two middle grade fantasy novels and is working on a Greek Mythology retelling. In her spare time, Ellen enjoys listening to K-pop, making her own clothes, and learning languages.

Joel Pank is an aspiring writer living in Cambridgeshire on the outskirts of Suffolk. He loves to write fiction in general, with science fiction being his favourite. Joel has A-levels in English Language, Theatre Studies, and Media Studies, as well as a BA (Hons) in English Literature and Creative Writing. He is currently studying for an MA in Creative and Critical writing at the University of Suffolk. Being an animal lover, Joel likes to take care of his four rescue cats: Jack, Clara, Maya, and Sox, as well as his Bearded Dragon,

Rufus. In his spare time, he likes to take walks around the countryside as not only does this ease his mind, but also gives him inspiration for his writing.

Muriel Moore-Smith is a writer and singer who lives in Suffolk with her husband and three daughters. She studied literature at several universities in the UK, completing an MA in Literature at the University of Essex before being lured to the sunny climes of California where she gained an MFA in vocal performance from the University of California, Irvine. She is currently studying for a PhD in Creative Writing at the University of Suffolk, where she is writing a historical fiction novel, *H's code,* based on the life of her great grandfather. A lover of stories in all their guises, Muriel is particularly interested in the opportunities writing presents to make sense of past lives and histories and the writer's obligations in this process.

Heather Rugg began her career as a mental health nurse in 1995 and then moved into nursing education in 2007. Heather has always been interested in the role education plays within social justice and has been rewarded by empowering others through her role as a nurse educator. In her career, Heather has worked with many service users and student nurses to achieve a sense of personal recovery and self-actualisation.

Heather is inspired by the lived stories of those she has journeyed with and would like to be a voice that challenges stereotypes and develops understanding and empathy. Heather began studying for an MA in Creative and Critical Writing to help develop the skills and attributes to enable her to tell the stories and capture imagination.

Jayd Green is a writer living in Norwich. She is currently a PhD candidate with the University of Suffolk, and Editorial Advisor for experimental poetry publisher, Osmosis Press. Her poems have appeared in *Anthropocene*, *Foliate Oak* literary magazine and *Royal Rose*, and *Footprints: An Anthology of New Eco Poetry* by Broken Sleep Books. Her writing and research are concerned with contemporary nature writing practices, ecocriticism, and the ecogothic.

Molly-Kate Britton completed her BA and MA at the University of Suffolk and is now a Creative Writing PhD student there. She is working on a novel about classical composer Alma Mahler-Gropius-Werfel. Her interests lie in historical fiction, as well as neo-gothic fiction, and the role of women within these genres. Her series, *Lives of the Wives*, sheds light on the women behind great men throughout history, and she has been published in several anthologies by the University of Suffolk.

Jessica Spence is currently taking her MA in Creative and Critical Writing at the University of Suffolk. Jessica dreams of one day being a prolific author. She enjoys reading and writing horror, fantasy, and sci-fi fiction.

Sarah Waterson is a postgraduate student currently completing the MA Creative and Critical Writing at the University of Suffolk. She has published a short story in the 2023 anthology *Suffolk Reflections*, and she is the co-editor of the 2024 anthology, *Suffolk Haunts*.

Rose Dawn is a doctoral researcher in English Literature at the University of Suffolk. Her project, 'Grief, Loss and

Hero-Worship in the Works of Branwell Brontë' explores the writing of the brother of the Brontë sisters, Branwell. Her research interests lie in Victorian literature, romantic poetry, and the Gothic. She is passionate about the heritage sector, which she shares through her position at Christchurch Mansion, as well as volunteering at the Brontë Parsonage Museum.

Alec Taylor has lived in Ipswich for most of his life. A career hiatus led Alec to return to education in his fifties, studying first Politics, and latterly an MA in Creative and Critical Writing at the University of Suffolk. Alec is currently working on a novel set between the Orwell and the Deben, amidst the aftermath of the *Tattingstone suitcases murder*, and the creation of Alton Water. Alec is no stranger to the Suffolk pubs, countryside and social life portrayed in his writing.

Chris Odogwu is a content creator from Nigeria. He has an interest in the business of publishing and film with hopes of creating opportunities for African creatives to tell authentic stories about the continent. Chris holds an MSc in Mass Communications, Public Relations, and Advertising from the University of Lagos and a BA in Mass Communications from the University of Jos. He is studying towards an MA in Creative and Critical Writing at the University of Suffolk.

Roy Haddock was born and raised in Ipswich, a child of the 1960s, hailing from a local council estate. He received no real formal education. A sickly child, he was away from school more than he was there. Given the opportunity to study for a Masters degree at sixty-one, he grabbed it with both hands. It has been an agonising journey for Roy to call himself a writer. Like a lot of writers, he has heard voices narrating stories in his head, but now he remembers them and makes sure to write them down. He hopes you enjoy this little bit of *squit*, as it is called in Suffolk. He dedicates his story to all those poor souls who have found their own form of bridge to leave this world and to all the loved ones who continue to fight their way through the darkness of grief.

Elise McManus completed her BA (Hons) English Literature with Creative Writing at the University of Suffolk. She is the 2023 recipient of the Suffolk Book League Dissertation Prize for English. She enjoys reading historical fiction and murder mysteries.

Amber Atkinson writes creatively and features her work in her Substack profile, *The Three Little Owls*. While currently working towards her MA in Critical and Creative Writing at the University of Suffolk, Amber has plans to further her interest in creative nonfiction through pursuing a PhD.

Caroline Roberts is a writer and freelance theatre maker based in Manningtree. She is passionate about women's voices and creative writing, and her special interest is the subject of motherhood in the works of Agatha Christie, which she is exploring through her PhD at the University of Suffolk. Caroline contributed a short story to *Suffolk Arboretum* (2022) and her rewriting of the 'Malekin' folk tale was published in *Suffolk Folk* (2021). She was shortlisted for the Student New Angle Prize (SNAP) in 2022 for her story 'The Manningtree Women.'

Mike Laurence is a retired GP living in South Norfolk. He is currently an MA student of Creative and Critical Writing at the University of Suffolk. His GP career was merely a fifty- year interlude between English A Level and his current studies, and he is enjoying lighting up areas of his brain that lay dormant for all that time.

Milena Ristic is a writer and translator from Serbia. She studied French literature for her BA and later pursued an MA in Public Relations and Communications. She is currently completing her MA in Creative and Critical Writing at the University of Suffolk. Her short stories have been published in her home country, but her real passions lie in cinema and theatre. She is hoping to write some good existential plays, maybe a screenplay or two and become a yoga instructor in the near future.

Jeni Neill: East Anglia is intrinsic to Jeni Neill, having spent her childhood in the Fens, formative years in Suffolk and then, later, settling with her own family in Norfolk. Four years ago, she felt driven to begin to write and form the ideas that had been brewing for many years, increasingly pressing for air. In 2020, she self-published *The Devil's Dye,* a locally set historical fiction novel. The following year, she produced a collection of short stories, *Fen Roads*, and enjoys giving talks about the creation of these books to local societies and libraries. She is currently studying on the MA in Creative and Critical Writing at the University of Suffolk, where course content and tutor guidance has helped identify her passion for both socio-political study and the fictional, magical realism. Her poem 'Winterton Pups' was shortlisted for the Student New Angle Prize 2023 and 'Colours of Our Days' won the SNAP prize

2024. Working from home, she cherishes time spent with her husband, four children and two grandchildren, as well as their modest menagerie of animals.

Lou Mary Carr is a writer living on the Suffolk/Norfolk border. She is studying on the MA Creative and Critical Writing at the University of Suffolk whilst caring for her two children and two cats. She is obsessed with the history, archaeology, and untold stories of the early Medieval era, and is currently writing a female-led epic set in seventh-century Northumbria and East Anglia. In her spare time, she volunteers with the Sutton Hoo Ship's Company at the Longshed in Woodbridge. She was runner-up in the Student New Angle Prize 2024.

Matthew Wiles is a writer living in Suffolk. He has written small fan works since 2017 and enjoys writing a mixture of science fiction and drama stories. Matthew is (as of this being written) studying for his MA in Creative and Critical Writing and was the winner of a scriptwriting award promoted by the University of Suffolk and sponsored by the New Wolsey Theatre. In his spare time, he enjoys listening to music and going on long walks, and lives at home with his dog, Murphy.

Rob Sadler is a poet and writer living in Suffolk. His poems have been included in various publications and exhibitions such as *House and Home*, *Mental Health Awareness Week*, *Metamorphosis*, and most recently *Suffolk Pride: We Are the One in Five.* He is currently studying on the MA Creative and Critical Writing course at the University of Suffolk and was shortlisted for the 2022 Student New Angle Prize.

He is currently adapting a series of memoirs into an autobiographical fiction novel set in and around his hometown of Ipswich. Rob enjoys acting, public speaking and long walks in the countryside with friends.

Sheena McCallum is a writer who grew up in various parts of rural Suffolk. The county holds many treasured memories from her younger years, tinged with the wilder Scottish influence of her father's side. She couldn't wait to leave Suffolk for the bright lights of Oxford's less prestigious university at eighteen, but was in so much of a hurry she rashly chose the first degree course her eyes fell on when opening the handbook. It took another three decades for Sheena to move back to Suffolk with her own family and to enrol on a course much closer to her heart; the MA in Creative and Critical Writing at the University of Suffolk. Sheena loves writing both poetry and prose, particularly memoir, and was shortlisted for the Student New Angle Prize 2024. Sheena has had poems published in Suffolk photographer Gill Moon's book *Planet Suffolk* and the Suffolk Writers Group's anthology *A Tapestry of Poetry*.

Tracy Davies is a mature student, and in an effort to improve her writing skills for her BA Counselling degree and reflective writing, Tracy decided to go back to her childhood comfort place of Shingle Street. It is a little-known stretch of the coast. Not famous like Orford, Aldeburgh, or Southwold, but that adds to its charm and wilderness.

While Tracy was there, she paused to reflect on how sadly the landscape has changed so dramatically, and that Tracy's daughter will never know it as she did. The result was the piece that Tracy wrote in her journal. Tracy then decided to enter the SNAP competition just for fun, never dreaming that she could ever be considered as a finalist. Tracy also hopes that she has inspired others not on English courses to also have a go and seize every opportunity that the University of Suffolk has to offer.

Harriet Sellers is an aspiring writer based in Suffolk. She has always been fascinated by words, inspired in part by her knowledge of Ancient Greek and Latin, which she studied as an undergraduate at the University of Oxford. Harriet is currently completing the MA Childhood Studies course at the University of Suffolk whilst also working in educational publishing and looking after her two young children. Originally from County Durham, she moved to Suffolk six years ago and enjoys exploring the region's scenic and gastronomic delights in her spare time.

Creative Writing at the University of Suffolk

The MA Creative and Critical Writing at the University of Suffolk offers you the opportunity to join a vibrant writing community and focus on your passion for creative writing whilst engaging with debates in critical theory. On the course, you will nurture and develop your skills as a writer, reader, and researcher. Enjoy a year-round guest speaker programme, author talks and publishing opportunities while broadening your knowledge of the production and reception of literature under the supervision of qualified academics and award-winning authors. To find out more please go to: https://www.uos.ac.uk/courses/pg/ma-creative-and-critical-writing

OTHER MA CREATIVE AND CRITICAL WRITING STUDENT ANTHOLOGIES AVAILABLE FROM THE TALKING SHOP PRESS

SUFFOLK FOLK:
East Anglian Folk Tales for the 21st Century.

In this collection of old tales re-visioned for contemporary readers, East Anglia's green children, mermaids, malekins and monsters come together with the secret lives of fairies and the power of lost-loves, making bold new stories that leap, hagstone in hand, into modern life.

'A wonderful collection of stories of Suffolk'
–Amazon 5* review

'A perfect gift in fact, for those with an interest in original short fiction, folk lore and Suffolk.'
–Waterstones 5* review

SUFFOLK ARBORETUM:
Original Stories Inspired by Remarkable Trees.

It is possible to find every tree or area of woodland featured in these stories. We recommend you take a tour of Suffolk with the anthology in hand and find each tree, from Haverhill to Lowestoft. Sit in the dappled shade of green canopies and read the original writing that our county's woodlands inspired.

SUFFOLK REFLECTIONS:
Original Stories Inspired by the Waterways of East Anglia

The stories in Suffolk Reflections run deep through our county's precious water reserves, its rivers, lakes, ponds, streams, and seascapes. This collection of new writing is a literary love song to water. From seal-skin selkies to the silver darlings of the herring fleets, from the beam of a lighthouse to flash floods and marshland ghosts, and a woman bathing in the starry glow of phosphorescence in a midnight sea, these original stories form a shifting tide of human stories of love and hope.

https://www.uos.ac.uk/study/ma-creative-critical-writing/

Join us!

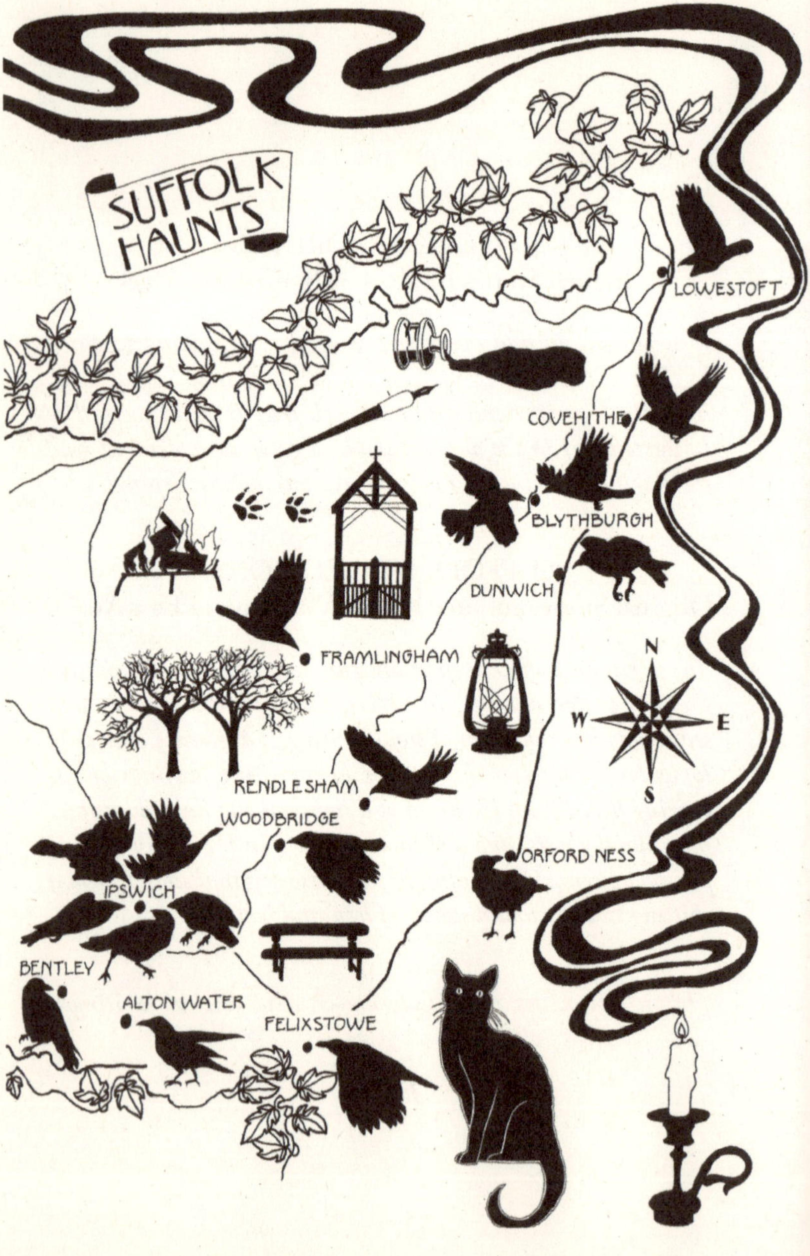
SUFFOLK HAUNTS
LOWESTOFT
COVEHITHE
BLYTHBURGH
DUNWICH
FRAMLINGHAM
N
W
E
S
RENDLESHAM
WOODBRIDGE
ORFORD NESS
IPSWICH
BENTLEY
ALTON WATER
FELIXSTOWE